Roni Denholtz

"Watch out," Sergei said. "There are icy spots here." He pointed to a big one not far from them.

"I see it," she said. She took a step towards her car and as she did, her foot slid on an unseen slick spot. Melissa tried to correct her balance.

Sergei grabbed her, preventing her from falling.

"Oh—" she leaned into him, then regained her balance. "Thanks." She placed her hands on his arms, slowly straightening. Her eyes met his brown ones. His mouth was near hers, and for a moment she wanted to kiss him.

Was she crazy?

DEDICATION

For My Friends Joan Soraka Waxman and Howard Waxman

Joan, we met freshman year at NSC in Folk Dance class, and we felt instant friendship.

Howard, after Joan met you, I sensed that you were meant for each other.

Here's to fifty plus years of friendship and many more!

ACKNOWLEDGMENTS

Many thanks to my niece, Lina Silber, for info on Russian traditions, food, etc. so I could make my story authentic. Any errors are my own.

Many thanks to my editor Judi Fennell for suggesting much-needed improvements to my story.

NOTE TO READERS

Some of you may recognize Melissa as Courtney's sister from *Lightning Strikes the Billionaire*. At the end of that book, Melissa had broken up with her boyfriend. But I knew I wanted to give her a happy ending eventually.

So when I decided to write another Hanukkah novella, Melissa stepped forward to be the heroine and I found a hero for her to love.

I do mention a few of the other characters from my award-winning *Lightning Strikes* series, but this book is independent of that series, not a part of it.

To learn more about the series, please visit my website at https://ronidenholtz.com/books/the-lightning-strikes-series

Whichever holiday you celebrate, I hope it's a wonderful one!

~ Roni Denholtz

CHAPTER I

Frozen snowflakes whirled in a furious dance. Piles of snow grew outside as Melissa Wallenberg stared out of her apartment window.

If this continued, school would be cancelled tomorrow. Not that a day off would be bad—her fourth-grade students were getting revved up for the holiday break and were bouncing off the walls already, despite its being early in December. She could use a day off, to wrap some Hanukkah and Christmas gifts for her friends and family, and to curl up with a cup of hot cocoa and a good book. Or shop on line. Although moving this past summer to her new apartment, new job and new school in a different state had been expensive, and she needed to watch her pennies. Fortunately, north-western New Jersey was cheaper than New York's Long Island, her former home.

She was as bad as the kids—hoping for a snow day.

The sound of a loud machine scraping snow had her turning to watch the large plow truck driving into the parking lot in front of her building.

Its lights lit up the beautiful but icy snow slanting down. Watching, she saw the truck zigzagging into a skid. She knew the vehicle wasn't supposed to slide that easily, but it did—right into the rear of her car!

"Shit!" she exclaimed, though there was no one to hear her. She lived alone.

The truck stopped, as if considering what had happened.

Before she could think further, she was stuffing her feet into her sturdy boots and pulling her coat on. Grabbing her keys and phone, she rushed down the stairs of her apartment and hurried outside.

Snow pelted her, the icy particles stinging her cheeks. She took a breath of the damp, cold air and waved.

"Hey! *Hey!*"

The driver had backed up the plow somewhat while she had grabbed her things and looked surprised that she was running towards him.

"That's my car you hit!" she yelled up to his cab.

He cracked open his window halfway. "I am sorry," he called back in a deep voice with the slightest hint of an accent. "My truck skidded. It is very icy tonight."

His English was a little stilted. She wasn't sure where that accent came from. Eastern Europe? Russia? Ukraine? It was slight, but after several years of teaching young children from various parts of the world, she could detect it.

He continued, "I would have left a note on your car, miss."

He shifted gears, then, leaving the truck idling, opened the door of the cab and jumped down to face her. "What is your apartment number? I'll leave my information there."

Wind hit them both, sending more icy particles against them. Melissa pulled her hood up.

"Or," he continued, "you can call the management and give them your information tomorrow, and I'll let them know what happened. I am truly sorry." His English sounded formal. She guessed again that it wasn't his first language.

"I'm in 12 B." She waved to indicate her doorway. "You can leave the note there."

"Again, I apologize. My company will pay for the damages, of course."

She looked at her small Nissan. The damage didn't appear too bad. There was a dent by her trunk, but fortunately it wasn't smashed in badly.

She focused on the guy for the first time. *Handsome*, she thought as she looked him over. He had brown eyes and light brown hair, a high forehead and broad shoulders which filled his black parka.

As she stared she caught the gleam of metal—a glint of gold by his neck. Was that a *star of David*?

He was Jewish… like her?

That surprised her. She had noticed most of the gardeners and workers in this apartment complex and the winter staff cleaning up snow chatted to each other in rapid Spanish.

She now felt compelled to help another Jew. "You must be freezing," she said. He wore no hat, only his thick puffy jacket and gloves. Of course she was not about to invite a total stranger into her apartment for a cup of hot coffee. She might not live in New York anymore, but she still had the typical common sense and wariness she'd grown up with. "Can I bring you out a hot drink? Coffee or instant cocoa?" she asked.

"Cocoa would be great." He smiled. "I don't want you to freeze out here. I could swing by when I finish the next two parking lots." He waved at the next building in the garden apartment complex.

"I'll have it ready in a few minutes," she told him, looking up at his attractive face. He was taller than her by at least six inches, and he appeared to be in good shape.

She wondered if he worked out or his build was from working outdoors, raking and shoveling etc. His smile was warm.

But who cared if he was good-looking? She wasn't looking for a guy. Why was she even noticing his features?

"12B, right?" he repeated.

"Yes." She started to turn. "I'll leave it in the vestibule."

"Thank you!" he called after her.

The wind buffeted her as she hurried back to her doorway.

Once inside the entryway, she unlocked her door and went up the interior stairs, shedding her coat. She proceeded to make a large mug of instant cocoa with little marshmallows floating in it. She tried not to think about *why* she felt so compelled to help this poor guy, who was working on a stormy night like this. *Because he's one of our people,* she told herself.

It certainly wasn't because she was looking to hook up with a Jewish guy. She had had plenty of offers to fix her up from well-meaning relatives during Thanksgiving at her sister Courtney's house this past weekend. She could still hear her aunts and cousins saying, "why on earth did you break up with that nice doctor you were seeing last year?" and "I have someone I'd like to introduce to you now."

She had had enough of match-making attempts. That was how she'd met Elliott, her former boyfriend. The guy who'd wanted a commitment but whom she just couldn't seem to love. The guy who'd then accused her of looking for perfection.

Elliott had been wrong. She had never been looking for perfection. She'd thought she'd had it once, and she'd had her dreams crushed. She had been left numb, and couldn't seem to care for anyone, including Elliott.

She'd made the tough decision to end her search for a future husband and just concentrate on being happy by herself—she was, after all, thirty-two—and move out to New Jersey and a more relaxed lifestyle. She was now nearer to her sister Courtney and her best friend from college, Rachel. She had decided to build a good life for herself. Alone.

She certainly had no intention of living like her cousin, Lori, waiting all the time for marriage, wondering if everyone she met was "the one."

She was startled when water began to boil in her teapot. Snapping back to reality, she shook out the envelope of cocoa mix and stirred it.

She couldn't help wondering about the man she'd met. He was handsome in an unpolished way—as if he didn't worry about looking good; just about being comfortable. Which, on a night like this, made perfect sense. Why would he go to the trouble of looking neat when he was in the middle of plowing snow?

The tempting smell of hot cocoa made her want to make some for herself too. She covered the mug she'd made for him so it stayed hot, and stirred another mug of mix for herself.

When she'd come home after Thanksgiving—relieved it hadn't been at her parents' home but at Courtney and her new husband Ben's home, so she didn't have to fight Long Island traffic or sleep at her parents' house—she'd been happier than she'd ever dreamed she would be to retreat to her cozy apartment. Away from her interfering relatives. She'd even begun decorating for Hanukkah to celebrate the holiday season. She'd posted a vertical *"Happy Hanukkah!"* sign on her door in the vestibule downstairs, and placed a plastic electric menorah on her windowsill in the front window.

Now, with the snow coming down, it truly felt like the holidays were near. And her apartment felt like home.

She looked but it didn't appear that he had finished her parking lot yet. She wandered back to her couch, wondering how long the guy would be before picking up his mug of cocoa.

Melissa considered calling Courtney. Or maybe her youngest sister, Sherry.

Deciding on Sherry, for no special reason, she clicked on her number. They spoke for a couple of minutes about the weather. Sherry, a lawyer, lived with her fiancé, also a lawyer, and they both worked in New York City. Their apartment was also in New Jersey but much closer to the city in trendy Hoboken.

"So I guess I'll see you in a couple of weeks at Mom and Dad's for the first night of Hanukkah," Sherry said, switching the topic.

"No, I'm not going," Melissa said firmly.

"*What?*" Sherry screeched.

"I'm not going," she repeated.

"Why not?"

"Because…" Melissa hesitated, not sure how to express all the emotions she was feeling. "It's such a hassle with traffic getting to Long Island."

"You could always go out the day before. Or you could come to our place and go with us. Or, I'm positive, Courtney and Ben would drive you. You always said you wouldn't miss a Hanukkah celebration—you enjoyed it so much."

"That was when I lived ten minutes from Mom and

Dad's house. But Thanksgiving wore me out, and last Hanukkah was awful, with everyone's prying into my life. Why had I broken up with Elliott, a nice Jewish doctor? All the aunts, cousins etc. wouldn't let up! Even at Courtney's wedding I was getting the same flak. I've had enough."

"Is *that* why you moved? Because you couldn't handle a few family members?" Sherry demanded.

"I have handled them. I moved because I wanted a fresh start," Melissa defended herself. "I was tired of the noise, the traffic, the constant scrutiny by my family. I wanted peace and quiet and whenever I visited my friend Rachel, I felt it out here." All true, which she had tried explaining to her family and friends many times. Rachel understood, and Melissa thought Courtney did too; but other family members didn't.

Regardless, she had looked for a new job, which she found in the same school where Rachel taught, not far from the place where her sister Courtney worked. Then she'd been able to find an apartment in a complex which was close to the school—and not far from the condo where Rachel lived with her fiancé.

Melissa loved her teaching job in the new town, and was equally happy with the choice she'd made of an apartment. It was a far cry from being isolated and in the boondocks as her mother had accused. The grocery only ten minutes away and there was less traffic than on Long Island. The stores were just as packed with merchandise and the parking was ample. She certainly wasn't "in the middle of nowhere," like her parents had said when Courtney moved out this way several years ago.

Now Melissa scooched further into the couch's cushions.

"I *like* it here, although you don't seem to believe that," she told her youngest sister. "I'm satisfied with my life." *And I don't need a man to complete it, she added silently.*

"Does this have something to do with Elliott?"

"No. I told you, I didn't love him even though we'd been seeing each other for a couple years. I didn't want to give him false hope that things would change. That would be unfair to him."

"So you cut him loose," Sherry said.

"Yes. We've had this conversation before. I thought you understood."

"I guess." Her sister didn't sound convinced

"Dad understands. So does Courtney. It's mother and our aunts who don't." Melissa could still hear her mother crying with disappointment. "But he's a doctor!" she'd sobbed. "He would be a wonderful son-in-law!"

"But not a husband—for me." Melissa had stood firm. "It's already done. I broke up with him," she had reiterated. She had broken up with Elliott *before* she told anyone.

Now she refocused on Sherry. "I don't want to discuss it again."

"Okay. But you could still come and see the rest of us for the first night of Hanukkah."

"No," Melissa said.

Melissa glanced at the window. Snow was still coming down. She could see lights pierce the area, and hear the plow turning into the parking lot. The guy must be back now for his cocoa. "I gotta go," she said to her sister. "I'm getting texts about school." It was a good excuse.

"Probably cancelled," Sherry said. "Enjoy your day off. I'll be working." She sounded almost jealous.

"Bye."

"Bye."

She got up and walked to the window. Sure enough, the plow had pulled into the parking lot and stopped near her car. The guy had done a pretty good job clearing the parking lot of snow, except for causing the dent to her car. And the way the wind was blowing the continuing snow, she was sure he'd be returning during the night.

She watched as he got out of his truck, and then she turned and went to her small kitchen to get the mug of cocoa.

The mug was still warm but not hot. Should she heat it for a few seconds in the microwave? Deciding to do that, she let it warm further, and was carrying it to her stairway which led to the front vestibule she shared with her downstairs neighbor when she heard the knock.

She carried it carefully with a potholder underneath, feeling the warmth in her palm.

"I'm coming!" she called cheerfully, and walked downstairs.

When she opened the door, the man stood in the vestibule by the outside door. He was even taller than she'd thought, and his broad shoulders took up a lot of the space in the area.

She shut her own door behind her.

The guy's face was undeniably attractive, with strong features and an easy grin. His light brown hair was windblown.

"Here." She thrust the mug at him. "Watch out. I just heated it up again."

"Thank you." He took it with his gloved hand and gave her a wide smile. "This is very kind of you, especially after I damaged your car."

"I know it was an accident," she admitted, and smiled too.

"It was." He blew on the cocoa.

Why was that sexy? She shoved the thought aside.

"I—What's your name?" she blurted.

"Sergei Rubenov. My friends call me Serge."

"Russian?" she asked.

"Yes. My parents came from there." He glanced outside through the main door's window. Snow continued to come down. He refocused on her. "What's your name?"

"Melissa." She felt comfortable sticking with first names. For now.

His eyes moved to the "Happy Hanukkah" sign she'd placed on her apartment door right after Thanksgiving.

"You celebrate Hanukkah?"

"Yes. You do too?" Once again she noticed the Jewish star resting in the V of his neck that flashed under her hall light.

"Yes. It's nice to see another Jewish person here. There aren't many in this complex."

She had observed a lot of Christmas décor in town and in her complex, even though Thanksgiving had just passed. "I like to decorate for the holiday," she told him. "Do you live here?"

"No. My brother and cousin and I have a house nearby."

"Nice." She wasn't sure what else to say, so she smiled.

"I better get going." He sounded reluctant. "Thanks so much for the hot cocoa, Melissa."

"You're very welcome."

"I'll drop off the mug later tonight. I'll leave it here

by the door," he said. "I'm sure we'll be plowing through the night, and I don't want to wake you."

"Okay," she replied.

He left, and she could hear him trudging through the snowstorm. She opened and shut the door and locked it behind her. She went back up her stairs. Walking to the window, she watched his truck pull away until the tail lights faded around the corner.

She sighed. He seemed like a nice guy. She'd probably never run into him again, unless she noticed him clearing the sidewalks of snow, or trimming hedges in the spring.

That thought was disappointing for some reason.

CHAPTER II

He'd finally met a girl who intrigued him, and it had been in weird circumstances.

He couldn't forget Melissa's pretty face or her cheerful expression.

Sergei plowed the parking lot next to Melissa's building. After that he had two more to do; then he and Dennis and Juan had to start blowing snow from the sidewalks before going to the next office job. And since the predictions were of snow throughout the night—and plenty of it--he'd have to do it all over again in the early morning hours. It would be an all-nighter for sure.

He sighed as he drove around to the next parking lot.

His thoughts strayed back to Melissa. She looked kind. He would like to get to know her better. But for all he knew, she was already involved with someone.

He hadn't been this intrigued by anybody since Tori. He sighed again.

***

Melissa expected a text any moment telling her school was cancelled tomorrow. What was the Superintendent waiting for? When she didn't get the text, she took a shower and got into old, comfy flannel PJs. She went to look out the window again and saw snow was still coming down. The snow drifts were starting to pile up and the parking lot would be covered with the soft snow again soon.

She wondered where Sergei was plowing now.

She yawned. The life of a teacher included getting up early, working hard all day with few breaks, and then taking work home you had to finish at night. She'd finished her grading and reviewing her plans, and her plans for next week had been turned in early, so she could relax. It wasn't even ten o'clock yet.

Her phone, sitting on the coffee table, pinged. She dashed over. Sure enough, the expected text was there: *No school tomorrow.*

Yay! A day off! She could wrap gifts, shop on line for more, watch movies and read. She was as happy as the kids. Although she enjoyed teaching, she'd been naïve about the difficulties when she began teaching ten years ago. And switching schools to teach in New Jersey had been an adjustment.

Plus she was teaching a new grade—fourth—and this was a new curriculum. The New Jersey schools didn't use the same materials as her school in New York did.

Which meant she'd been working very hard.

She decided to have a glass of wine to celebrate. Normally she didn't drink during the week except for Fridays.

As she sipped her chardonnay, she glanced outside again

The wind was blowing snow. She thought about Sergei braving the elements on this cold, snowy night, making the streets safe for people like her.

She sighed and took her book off the coffee table, immersing herself in the regency romance she'd started reading a couple of days ago. It was one of a bunch of books she'd been stockpiling to read when she had the chance.

By eleven she was tired. She got up at 6 AM normally to get ready for the school day, so she'd been awake a long time. And the kids were always hyper in December, right before the holidays, especially if they thought they might get a day off from school. Her patience had worn thin today.

She got ready for bed, adding her extra blanket to her soft comforter. She read for a few more minutes, then turned off her night stand lamp and closed her eyes. With a day off tomorrow, she didn't need to set her alarm.

Her mind drifted. She missed having someone next to her to hold her and warm her. She didn't miss her boyfriend Elliott, per se, only the comforting presence of a man. Elliott had filled in as a steady presence in her life for over two years.

"I didn't want to string him along," she'd told her family when they'd been shocked and upset by her break-up. "It isn't fair to him. He's a nice enough guy, but after two years I don't feel any more than a casual caring about him. Certainly not love." She didn't mention that sex had just been ho-hum.

Her entire family thought she was nuts. Except for her next younger sister, Courtney, who was twenty-nine now, three years younger than Melissa. Courtney, who'd married her soul mate, understood Melissa's yearning for a strong love and commitment.

And if Melissa couldn't find it, she wouldn't settle for less. She'd just live her life the best she could.

Brad crossed her mind.

She thought back to Brad, her first love—her boyfriend in college and for a time afterwards. Brad was majoring in finance and had become a Wall Street type.

His family had money, so her mother loved him. So did Melissa, but not for that reason. Brad had been hot, attentive—and the sex was great. She'd been hopelessly in love with him. But after more than two years he hadn't shown any commitment.

Then she found out why. She'd gone to surprise him on the first night of Hanukkah at his apartment—opened the unlocked door to a shock—he was having sex with another woman on the living room couch She was a gorgeous blonde, from a wealthy Long Island family, and had both looks and money. And power. Melissa had found all this out too late. And Brad had been seeing her on the nights Melissa had believed he was working late, or getting together with "the guys" he knew from college who also lived in the City now.

She'd been shocked. Heart-broken. The man she was sure she would marry had been cheating on her for, it turned out, nearly six months—and she hadn't had any clue. None. And when she found him entangled with Kyla, stark naked, she had thought she wanted to die.

Caught in the act, at least Brad hadn't lied. He'd admitted the truth, and told Melissa that during the last few months, what had started as pure attraction for them had turned into love. He was going to get engaged to Kyla. He just hadn't gotten around to telling Melissa.

Melissa, shocked and devastated, had somehow made it to the train station and back home to her own apartment.

Then, the anger came, followed by more hurt and betrayal. He'd lied to her for months. He'd *used* her. She was a convenient girlfriend, there when Kyla was unavailable, dependable when Kyla wasn't handy for screwing.

Melissa had walked away from Brad.

She'd read about his engagement on social media a few weeks later. Then, the following year, in which she'd hardly dated, about their big wedding. The photos she saw on-line still pierced her.

After that, Melissa hadn't trusted anyone.

Now she turned in her bed to a different position.

Elliott, kind and dependable Elliott, had come along—but he was simply someone to spend time with. She hadn't loved him, not the way a girlfriend should, despite trying. So last year she'd let him go. She refused to use him the way she'd been used. Elliott was a kind man and deserved love.

She had enjoyed the sex. If not thrilling like it had been with Brad—sex with Elliott was at least decent. She'd enjoyed the intimacy and comfort of having a man close to her.

She turned over again.

She wasn't ever giving her heart away again. But she had to admit to herself that she missed having a good sexual relationship.

Maybe she needed to find a "friend with benefits."

Sergei's image flashed in her mind. She turned over again.

No, no, she chided herself. She knew better than to go out with some unknown man. Stories of creeps appeared on the news all the time. She couldn't take that chance.

But she could still imagine. For a minute, she pictured his large hands cupping her face, then sliding down her arms. She grew warm. Opening her eyes, she turned over again and ordered herself to go to sleep. But it took a while.

CHAPTER III

Melissa slept late, then had a leisurely breakfast and shower. She could savor having the day off, and she spent the morning wrapping Hanukkah and Christmas gifts to music on her phone app. By noon she had done all of the gifts she had already purchased and made notes about the ones she had yet to buy.

Then she called Rachel, curling up on her bed, a seasonal cinnamon-scented candle lit on her dresser. She told Rachel about meeting Sergei.

"Is it weird that I've been having fantasies about a good-looking stranger?" she asked, half joking, half serious.

"Not at all," Rachel replied staunchly. "You haven't been with a man for a long time. Fantasies are normal! Are you going to see him again?"

"I was going to go see the management about the insurance claim later when the roads are completely clear. Or maybe I'll walk. The building isn't too far away. I'll ask for his contact info."

"Find out what you can," her friend encouraged. "Are we still meeting to shop tomorrow?"

"As long as the roads are okay. I should be able to finish my shopping then."

"See you at noon at the usual place in the mall."

When she got off the phone, Melissa glanced outside her window. The snow now sparkled under the bright blue sky.

She should probably go clean off her car and check her front door for Sergei's info.

She got into her heavy winter coat and pulled on a warm hat, boots and gloves. When she opened her inner door, she saw the paper sticking underneath her mug in the vestibule. His name and phone number and the information on his vehicle insurance were on an attached business card, along with the message, "I'm very sorry."

Sergei Rubenov.

She pictured him last night. He'd been true to his word and left her all his contact info.

After placing the mug and paper back on a step in her apartment, she walked outside.

Surprise struck her. Her car had been totally cleaned off. The front and back windshields, the side windows, even the wipers had been cleared of all the snow and ice.

Plus, someone had shoveled beside the tires of her car, so she didn't have to do that herself. She'd be able to pull out of her parking space easily.

It must have been Sergei. She couldn't think of any neighbor who'd do that for her. She had only been here a few months, and didn't know her neighbors that well, except for the older woman downstairs; and Melissa was certain she hadn't done this.

She stood there, a warm pleasant feeling weaving through her body. How considerate of him!

She impulsively wanted to call and thank him. But he'd probably worked all night, and was sleeping now. She'd call tomorrow, she decided.

Instead, she warmed up her car for a few minutes,

then shut it off. The roads appeared clear now. She should be able to finish her shopping at the mall tomorrow.

She walked to the apartment complex office through neatly cleared pathways, pleased that Sergei seemed so honest. She had figured she would be the one to have to report the accident.

When she arrived at the office, the middle-aged secretary on duty nodded her head when Melissa gave her name and apartment number. "Oh, yes, Sergei informed us."

"He seems very nice and honest," Melissa remarked.

The woman—Jean something--nodded again. "A real gentleman."

Melissa was tempted to ask if Jean knew any more about Sergei, but resisted. He must have been a good worker if the complex used his services.

The woman studied Melissa. "We like his company," she volunteered. "They're dependable."

"That's good," Melissa said.

As she trudged back to her apartment, she thought about Sergei again. Too bad she didn't have more information about him. She guessed he was about her age.

When she went to bed that night, after a quiet and relaxing day, Melissa found herself thinking about him again. She imagined lying here with him, touching him…

***

The following morning Melissa was having coffee when she decided to call Sergei and thank him for cleaning off her car.

She called her insurance company first, and gave them all the info.

She expected to get Sergei's voicemail. He'd probably

be resting all weekend after the hours he'd put in on Thursday overnight. But he picked up on the second ring.

"Rubenov Company," he said. "This is Sergei Rubenov."

"Sergei? This is Melissa. Melissa Wallenberg. I wanted to thank you for cleaning off my car the other night."

"No problem," he declared. Then, "did you say Wallenberg?"

"Yes, I did."

"Any relation to Courtney?"

He knew Courtney? "She's my middle sister," she told him. "Do you know her?"

"Yes," he replied. "We do the snowplowing and landscaping at The Lightning Center. I've met the whole staff."

"Oh!" That meant she could speak to Courtney, find out more about this attractive stranger, and feel safe if she saw him again. "That was so nice of you to clean off my car."

"It was the least I could do, after hitting your car. The truck slid. I'm really sorry."

"It will get fixed," she reassured him.

"Well, you let the insurance company follow up."

"Of course. How are you doing?"

"Fine. Thanks for asking." He hesitated.

She wanted to invite him over for a cup of coffee, but quelled that idea. Invite a strange man into her home? Her parents and friends would be screeching at that. Instead, she asked, "Can I meet you at the local Panera and buy you a cup of coffee?"

"I'd like that. But let me buy you a cup."

"We can fight about it when I see you," she said,

smiling even though he couldn't see it. "I'm meeting a girlfriend to go shopping today. How about tomorrow?"

"That's perfect. I know where the local Panera is. What time?"

They could do lunch. "Twelve noon?"

"Yes." He sounded enthusiastic.

"Ok, I'll see you then."

"Bye," he said, and clicked off.

With an eye on the clock, she showered and got dressed. The mall was always crowded on Saturdays, especially just before the holidays, and she was due to meet Rachel at eleven.

Once in her car, she put in a call to Courtney while on blue tooth.

Courtney answered promptly, and Melissa asked her about Sergei and Rubenov Brothers.

"Oh, yeah, I've met him and his brother and cousin," her sister told her. "They're all nice guys. They've been working for The Lightning Center for over a year." The Lightning Center was a facility nearby, the top center for research on people who had developed psychic powers after being struck by lightning. Courtney was a researcher there.

"What do you know about him?" Melissa quickly explained about his truck sliding on the ice into her car.

"Well, he seems very honest," Courtney remarked. "I know that he and his brother and cousin are hard-working guys. And their staff is always courteous. They handle any requests that Parker asks them to do. Like everyone who works here or for the Center, Matt—our security consultant—completely checked them out. No red flags."

"He's quite attractive," Melissa said as she merged onto the Interstate.

"Is that interest I hear?" Courtney asked.

"A little. You know I'm not looking for anything serious."

"I know." Courtney sighed. "Yes, he *is* handsome. So are his other family members. And Sergei is unattached as far as I know."

"Maybe I would enjoy his company," Melissa said lightly. "Like a friendly relationship. I'm meeting him for lunch."

"Have a good time!" Courtney sounded a little too enthusiastic.

"Don't make a big deal about it," Melissa cautioned.

"I won't."

"I'm going shopping now with Rachel," Melissa said. "I'm almost at the mall. I'll talk to you soon."

"Okay. Bye. I'm going shopping too, with Priscilla and Lindsay." Those were two of her sister's friends from work. Melissa had met them before.

"You could join Rachel and I," she invited. "We'll be at Rockaway Mall."

"Oh, sorry. We're going to the Mall at Willowbrook. Lindsay's never been to that one."

"Have fun!" They said their goodbyes, and Melissa disconnected.

As she exited the Interstate, she couldn't help thinking about Sergei. What would he look like underneath all those heavy winter clothes? She had seen him around during the summer and gotten a glimpse of a broad chest and shoulders. The thought of wrapping her arms around them was too appealing. She shut down those thoughts and she drove slowly, looking for a parking space.

Since they were meeting early, the mall was busy with holiday shoppers but not yet jammed. She'd already purchased gifts like candy and candles for school aides and secretaries and a colorful scarf for Rachel, plus nice sweaters for her mother, father and brother-in-law, Ben. Now she needed gifts for her two sisters and for her youngest sister's fiancé, Dave.

She met Rachel and they shopped first in the large department store. She bought designer purses for both her sisters since they liked them. It was a stretch to pay for those, but she knew they'd be happy with the gifts. Then she found a sports sweatshirt for Dave.

Rachel was finishing buying a warm hat for her own dad. Once done with that store, they dropped their purchases in their cars then headed back into the mall to the food court. Holiday music played in the background and they selected the Chinese food place.

Once seated, Melissa asked her friend what else she wanted to buy.

"I want to go into Victoria's Secret," she said. "My friend Allie likes a certain perfume they carry. Besides, I'd like to select a new nightgown for me."

Melissa grinned at her friend. Now she wanted her opinion. "You hinted I need a friends-with-benefits relationship?"

"When you're between guys—I know that's your choice—a casual fling can fill the time," Rachel said, digging into her lo mein.

"That's not like me," Melissa pointed out.

"I know. But the other night you sounded lonely for male companionship. It could fill the void."

"I'll think about it. Melissa changed the subject to Rachel's wedding this summer. Then they headed to the store.

While Rachel browsed, Melissa did too. She found a cologne she liked and decided to splurge, hoping she wouldn't regret the bill. She also looked at the wide array of nightgowns. She really didn't need one, but a beautiful emerald green nightgown of satiny fabric caught her eye. She could just imagine wearing it with Sergei… she found herself flushing. *Whoa. Stop.* There was no guy in her life right now.

"Go ahead and buy it," Rachel said. "You never know when you'll be able to use it."

Melissa fingered it again, then, giving into the impulse, took the skimpy nightgown to the register along with the cologne.

She really didn't need either, but here she was, buying both.

She had fun shopping with Rachel. They went into several stores, browsing, and she finished her list with a gift for her favorite cousin. When she and Rachel parted, she drove home, smiling and singing along with the holiday music on the radio.

She liked living here in New Jersey in this less congested part of the state, away from the status-conscious and crowded area where she'd grown up, and had previously worked. The only bad thing that had happened since she moved out here—and it had been small—was the accident involving Sergei's truck and her car.

Once home, Melissa lugged her gifts inside in two trips, made herself a cup of coffee and wrapped the presents while she sipped. Finally, with yesterday's and today's piles of presents nearby, she sat down and opened the book she was reading by a favorite author.

She immersed herself until she felt hungry and glancing up, saw it was nearly seven o'clock, and went to warm up some soup.

The evening passed quietly.

Alone in her bed, she couldn't help thinking about Brad again and the many nights she had snuggled up with him. And Elliott, although her feelings for him hadn't been deep.

She missed that male companionship and good sex, which she'd definitely experienced with Brad. She turned and flipped her pillow. There was still an ache in her heart, even now, years later, for the love she'd had for Brad. The love that had been betrayed so badly.

Various relatives had offered to set her up with men, after the fiasco with Brad; but for a while she had no desire to date. A few months later, she started going out again, cautiously. She'd met Elliott at a friend's party, and felt comfortable with him. Until a few years later she'd realized he'd grown serious and she didn't feel the same.

Her move and new job meant she was starting with a clean slate. She probably should have done it before this past summer.

And, she vowed, she would never get into the kind of relationship again that she'd had with Brad. Never crazily in love again. She would get used to a life by herself, and make the best of it. And if the opportunity for a wild fling came along, well, hey, maybe she'd take it. She'd have some fun.

CHAPTER IV

Melissa wanted to be prompt, so she arrived a few minutes before noon. Wind buffeted her as she entered the building and pulled off her gloves.

Even though she was early, she spotted Sergei already at a table by one of the windows. He'd draped his heavy navy jacket over a chair, reserving it for her, she guessed. He wore a red sweater and jeans.

The smell of freshly-brewed coffee hung in the air. The place was crowded, mostly with shoppers, checking their phones and lugging bags from local shops.

She'd worn a newer pair of jeans and a black sweater patterned with shite snowflakes. She liked looking festive and seasonal.

"Melissa," he called out and waved.

She moved towards his table, placing her coat on the chair. "Hey, Sergei. I'll order. What do you want?"

He stood up, and she realized he was even taller than she recalled. Probably 6' 1 or 2. His shoulders were broad. With his brown, wavy hair and dark eyes, and high cheekbones, he was a lot handsomer than most of the men eating nearby. Women in the eatery were studying him.

"What do you want?" she repeated.

"I know you offered," he protested, "but please let me buy the food. I was the one who damaged your car."

"But you were up front about it, and you shoveled and cleaned it off," she said, "so please allow me."

"No, I insist," he reaffirmed.

Melissa gave in. She didn't want to argue, since he was being so nice. She ordered a plain coffee, a healthy Greek salad and a sugar cookie shaped like a snowman just to indulge a bit. Sergei ordered plain coffee too, a sandwich and two cookies. He paid and then she went to add milk and sweetener to her coffee.

He came up beside her but left his coffee black, adding only sugar. They went back to their table and sat down.

She thanked him again, then started the conversation. "My sister sees you at work sometimes."

"Your sister Courtney?"

"Yes. I guess you know that she works as a researcher at The Lightning Center."

"We do their landscaping, and snow plowing," Sergei said. "I was there the other night."

"I know, she mentioned that." She stirred her coffee, then inhaled the roasted aroma. "I love the smell of coffee."

"I do too. It keeps me going during those long nights."

"Do you always do the plowing yourself? Courtney says you own the business with your relatives."

"My brother Dennis and our cousin Victor. We have quite a few employees. On nights like the other night when it was snowing so much, one of us always supervises the guys. But Juan was out with the flu all week, so I filled in for him, plowing."

She was curious about his business. "How long have you had your business?" She didn't want to appear too nosy, so she added, "I'm interested in small businesses."

"It will be five years in March," he said. "My brother Dennis and I like the outdoors, and kicked around the idea for a while. Victor always had an interest in plants, and he studied botany in college. Dennis and I were business majors, so we brought that perspective to the business."

She hadn't known he went to college. She shouldn't make assumptions, she told herself, just because she saw him trimming some bushes or snow plowing. "Where did you go to school?"

"We all went to Rutgers. How about you? What do you do, and where'd you go?"

"I went to one of the SUNY's," she said, referring to the state university system in New York. "I studied elementary education. I teach fourth grade."

"My sister, Tatiana is a teacher. Chemistry," he added. "I know teaching is a hard job."

"Yes, it is; but fulfilling too," she added. "I love the kids."

"Have any of your own?"

She shook her head. "I've never been married."

His mouth dropped open slightly. "I'm surprised," he said frankly. "You're so pretty, and friendly."

She felt her face flush. "Thank you."

"I mean it."

Dishes and utensils clinked nearby as she stared at him. "How about you?"

"No. I haven't met the right woman."

An uneasy silence fell. Wanting to fill it, she asked, "where do you live?"

"Dennis and I bought a house in Stanhope a couple of years ago." That was a town close to hers. "We're less than an hour from our families--and Victor lives with his girlfriend in Flanders."

"So my apartment complex is near where you live," she concluded.

"Yes. In fact, we all lived in the apartments there when we started our business," he told her. "At the time they weren't landscaped as nicely, so we got the job when we started out."

She sensed he was trying to impress her. Why? she wondered. Did he care about her opinion? Apparently so.

"Did you always live in this area?" she asked.

"No. We grew up in Fairlawn."

It was a popular area in Bergen county, more crowded and with more expensive homes, she knew. It wasn't too far from where Courtney and her husband lived now.

"My parents have lived there ever since they came to this country," he continued.

"Where did they come from?" she asked, curious.

"Russia. I was born here in the USA."

"Tell me about your family," she urged.

"I'm the third kid of the family. Dennis is the baby." He grinned. "My cousin is in between the two of us. I'm thirty-two, Victor is thirty-one, and Dennis is thirty. How about you—where are your people from?"

"My father's grandfather came from Russia," she told him. "My mother's family from Austria-Hungary. An area that was sometimes claimed by Austria, sometimes Hungary."

"Do you know what part of Russia they came from?" he leaned forward.

She shook her head. "I could ask my dad if he knows. I know that my grandfather was a toddler when they came over, but he passed a couple of years ago." She sipped her coffee. It was still hot, so she stirred it again.

"My people were from St. Petersburg."

"I can ask my dad," she said. She realized that was implying she wanted to see him again. So she added, "if you really want to know."

"Yes, I'd be interested in learning that," he affirmed, polishing off his sandwich.

They ate in silence for a few minutes as customers all around them spoke animatedly. Melissa speared a piece of grilled chicken on top of her salad. Sergei bit into one of his cookies, shaped like a tree and iced in green. "Mm, this is good. Sweet."

She finished her salad, then sampled her snowman cookie. Then she added, "I'm the oldest of three girls."

He raised his eyebrows. "No boys?"

"No. But my dad always says he loves his girls," she added. It was true. Her dad had never complained about having only girls. That is, she had never heard him complain.

"How about you?" she asked.

"Two sisters. Tatiana and Fania were born in Russia. Dennis and I were born here."

"I'm thirty-two also," she offered.

"Yeah? When's your birthday?"

"Beginning of July. And you?"

"January 4th."

"So you're a Capricorn, like Courtney."

They spoke about the zodiac for a few minutes. Sergei said his mother discounted "that stuff."

"I find it fascinating," Melissa admitted. "My mother doesn't believe in it either." She sipped more coffee, which had cooled to a much more tolerable temperature. "But Courtney is also fascinated. She is really into past lives."

"That's interesting," he said. "I understand they're

doing some ground-breaking research in psychic phenomena over there at The Lightning Center."

"Yes. It makes me wish I had a psychic ability," Melissa admitted.

"You seem fine the way you are." He gave her an admiring look.

She warmed at his words, despite wondering if that was just a line. Out loud she said, "You seem fine just the way you are too."

He grinned. "Thanks." He sipped coffee too. "Do you have any hobbies?"

"I love to read," she answered. "How about you?"

"Besides liking plants, I like to play chess. My father taught me to play when I was young."

"Really?" She knew only a few people who played.

"I also like to play poker," he added. "I play with Victor and a couple of his friends."

"Your brother doesn't like to play?"

"No, he doesn't care for cards," Sergei said. "But I do. We play for a few dollars just to make it a challenge."

"I haven't played cards since college," she said. "But I do enjoy doing some crafts. Once in a while my youngest sister, Sherry, and I will do a craft together—like making decorations for Courtney's bridal shower. That was fun."

He asked her about music she liked, and told her he liked country western music. Melissa was surprised. "I mostly listen to today's pop artists. But I do enjoy music."

"There's going to be a country group playing at the Town Theatre on Friday. Want to come with me?"

His voice sounded eager. It could be fun, she thought. "Yes," she said. "It sounds like fun. I do enjoy many kinds of music. I was in chorus all through school."

"How about we go out to dinner before?" he asked. "There's a pretty good restaurant that just opened in Netcong. I went there with Dennis last week and they have a great selection of food."

She'd have a chance to get to know him better before the concert, and decide if she wanted to see him again. He seemed nice and he was definitely attractive. Aloud she said, "I'd like that."

They chatted for another half hour, and as the place grew more crowded and people were searching for tables, she suggested they leave. "This was fun," she finished. "I'm looking forward to the concert Friday."

"I am too. Pick you up at 5:30?"

"That's fine." They exchanged phone numbers.

They left the coffee place and stepped into the sunny but cold afternoon. Wind struck hard, and Melissa pulled on her gloves.

"Watch out," Sergei said. "There are icy spots here." He pointed to a big one not far from them.

"I see it," she said. She took a step towards her car and as she did, her foot slid on an unseen slick spot. Melissa tried to correct her balance.

Sergei grabbed her, preventing her from falling.

"Oh—" she leaned into him, then regained her balance. "Thanks." She placed her hands on his arms, slowly straightening. Her eyes met his brown ones.

His mouth was near hers, and for a moment she wanted to kiss him.

Was she crazy? She hardly knew him. She felt herself flushing. She was oh-so-aware of his muscular body. The spark of attraction she felt made her feel more off-balance than the moment before, when her boot had started to slide on the ice.

She took a cautious step back. "I'm okay now, thanks."

"No problem." He regarded her.

She stepped carefully and made it to her car without a misstep. "I'll see you Friday," she said in a light tone. "Thanks for lunch!"

"It was my pleasure." It sounded like he meant it, she thought when she got into her car. They waved at each other, and then she started for home.

Her thoughts whirled. She hadn't felt this—spark, this attraction, for a long, long time.

She wouldn't worry about it. One date wouldn't make a difference in the scheme of things. It wasn't as if she intended to have a serious relationship with *anyone*.

CHAPTER V

"How do you dress if you are thinking of seducing someone?" Melissa wondered in a low voice as she and Rachel left the school Friday afternoon.

"Appropriately for the occasion—jeans for a concert--but with a sexy top," her friend suggested. "And sexy underwear," she added.

Melissa laughed. "Sounds like good advice."

She drove home. But she stopped at a pharmacy, where she did something she'd never done before--bought a small package of condoms. Now she could feel free to enjoy herself if the opportunity came up.

As soon as she returned home, she dropped the package into her nightstand drawer.

She took a quick shower. It was a casual date, she reminded herself as she got dressed. Besides, she didn't own a lot of sexy clothes. She hadn't for a long time.

She'd had a lot sexy outfits when she went with Brad. But that chapter of her life was firmly closed.

Now she pulled out several drawers and rummaged through her closet before she found just what she wanted. She dressed in a lacy bra and bikini, and then put on nice jeans and a V-neck pink top. She added her simple gold necklace with a Jewish star.

***

"Where you going?" Sergei's brother asked, as Sergei pulled on his jacket. Before he could answer, Dennis added "Want to go hear that band at the Town Theatre?"

"Sorry, bro," Sergei answered. "I'm already going… with a date. I mentioned that yesterday." His brother could be absent-minded.

"Yeah? With who?" Dennis eyed him.

"That girl I told you about last weekend. I like her," Sergei reminded him.

Dennis' mouth dropped open. "You mean the one whose car you dented?"

"It wasn't intentional. And she doesn't seem to hold it against me."

Dennis narrowed his eyes. "Maybe she will and you don't realize it yet."

"I don't think so." At least, he hoped not. It was rare for him to feel such a sudden, intense attraction to someone. "I want to get to know her better. She seems a lot different than Tori." Tori had been more lively—but look what had happened with *that*.

"I should hope so. You don't want a repeat of that disaster," Dennis said.

Tori had been Sergei's girlfriend three years ago and he'd really cared for her. Apparently it wasn't the same for her. She had dumped him when she learned that his mother couldn't help her fledgling art career. She had *used* him.

"Have fun," his brother called after him as Sergei opened the front door.

"I intend to."

***

She was ready when Sergei arrived promptly at 5:30.

They went to dinner at a casual American restaurant. Knowing they'd be drinking at the club, she declined wine. But the meal was good and she enjoyed Sergei's company. They discussed music they liked; and a bit about their childhoods. Melissa learned Sergei had grown up speaking both English and Russian. She had already noticed he spoke with barely any accent. He'd also studied French in high school.

"I took Spanish," she told him.

"Did you ever go to Spain?" he asked.

"My best friend Rachel and I visited Spain and Portugal a couple of years ago," she said.

"I visited Russia with my whole family twice when I was younger. We went to see some elderly relatives; but my parents prefer not to go back now that those family members have passed."

"Where else have you traveled?"

"I went to Cancun, Mexico on a spring break with some college buddies," he said. He leaned towards her. "And I went on one of those trips to Israel that's for college students. Did you ever do that?"

"Yes," she said. "It was fascinating. What did you like best?"

"Seeing the ancient sites."

They discussed several of the places they'd seen on their Israeli trips. They agreed on some of the must-see places they'd visited.

"I'd love to travel again," Melissa said. "Especially since I don't always work in the summer, unless I can work in a special summer program but they're usually short. A couple of summers I've picked up jobs at stores in the Mall. It gave me extra spending money."

He reached out and took her hand. A warm thrill went up her arm straight to her insides.

"I know you teachers work hard and don't get paid as well as you should," he said. His voice and face were solemn.

"Yes," she agreed. Her voice came out breathy. "We do work hard and many of us have to work summers to make ends meet."

"I know Tatiana usually has to take work home with her, even on weekends," Sergei added. "Do you do that, Melissa?"

"Yes." She nodded. She was glad he recognized the important work she did. He had obviously observed the hours his sister put in on the job.

She liked him, she decided. He was a nice guy. And with the reference from her sister Courtney, the idea of seduction was a distinct possibility.

She got the impression that he enjoyed their dinner. She relaxed as they ate and talked. If she was going to have a fling it should be with someone whose company she enjoyed, she told herself.

When they went to the nearby club, it was already getting busy. Sergei asked her what she wanted to drink, and she chose a peach martini. Sergei ordered a vodka martini.

The opening band was just so-so, she thought. The main band took the stage to a lot of applause. She didn't know much about country western music, but did recognize when they played "Achy Breaky Heart." Some of the people in the crowd sang along. After listening to a couple of songs, including one they'd written recently, she decided she liked them.

"They're really good," she said loudly to Sergei so he could hear her over the noise of the crowd.

"I agree," he said, and slung his arm around her, warming her insides again.

She let her glance rove over his handsome face and broad shoulders.

"They're even better than I expected," he said, sipping his drink.

During a slow song they joined others on the dance floor. Sergei pulled her close and Melissa nestled against his hard body. *Wow, he really was built.* She could feel his taut muscles under his clothes. She liked the sensation of being held against his masculine body. Sparks lit all over her feminine one.

He tightened his hand holding hers. When the song ended, they returned to their table and he moved his chair closer. When the band finished, he asked if she wanted to stay. She shook her head. It had been a long day. They both got to their feet.

He drove carefully and steadily back to her apartment while they chatted about the songs they'd enjoyed the most.

Would he want to make love? she wondered. She was totally attracted to him, and she had definitely enjoyed their date.

Once he pulled into her parking lot, she asked "Want to come in for a soda or another drink?"

"Yes." He smiled.

"What do you want to drink?" she asked him when they were inside and had gone up her interior stairs into the living room. They shed their coats and she slid off her boots and invited him to do the same.

"Coffee?" he asked.

"Ok, I can make some. I'll have cocoa," she added. "I can't drink coffee this late."

"In that case, I'll take the same."

"It's instant," she warned.

"That's fine," he said, smiling.

They sat on her couch and sipped their cocoas as the tiny marshmallows bounced on top.

What should she do next? She wanted to make herself seem available to him, but she didn't want to throw herself at him. That would be too embarrassing, like she was desperate or something. Besides, she was unsure how he felt. She hoped that he found her attractive.

But what if he wasn't interested in taking things further? In her limited experience, most guys leaped at the chance to have sex. But she didn't know Sergei well enough to assume that.

Well, there was only one way to find out.

She set her mug on the coffee table with a loud clink. After a charged second, in which she tilted her head up and smiled at him, he did the same, smiling back. She focused on his mouth.

He slid closer.

"Melissa." He hesitated.

She scooted closer. "Yes?" she asked in a breathless voice.

He pulled her into his arms, and kissed her on the lips.

The kiss started out gently. She kissed him firmly, enthusiastically, and after a moment she slid her hands around his neck.

His tongue dove inside her mouth, tasting of sweet cocoa and the liquor he'd had. She pressed herself closer. Their tongues tangled, and she heard him groan. His fingers speared her hair.

Sparks cascaded all over her entire body. In that moment she knew she *wanted* him. Wanted his hands all over her.

After a minute he pulled back a little.

"Melissa—" he was almost out of breath— "if we don't stop. I may be getting ideas you're not comfortable with—"

"Believe me, Sergei," she said, breathless herself, "I'm comfortable with your ideas." She proved it by bringing his head back down to hers and kissing him.

He tightened his grip on her, whispering "I want you, Melissa," as he kissed her cheek, her forehead, then her mouth again. "And I have protection."

She was happy to hear that. She'd been unsure how to tell him that she had some.

"I'm so attracted to you—" he cupped her cheek.

"I feel the same." To prove her point, she kissed him hard again.

His response was instantaneous. He pulled her closer, locking her against him.

They slid into a prone position. His body felt wonderfully masculine beside hers. She instinctively thrust her hips towards him. She could feel the bulge in his jeans

After a minute of kissing, she pulled her head back and regarded him with a smile. "You're so considerate to ask me so politely." He was definitely a thoughtful person.

She moved out of his arms and stood up on shaky legs. She extended her hand and pulled him up beside her. *Was she really doing this? Yes, she was making it clear she wanted him.*

The desire she felt for him was all-encompassing. "C'mon." She gave a tug, and he followed her.

She led him to her bedroom and turned on a low light. Then she sat on the bed and patted it.

He sat beside her, smiling. Then he gathered her in his arms.

Sergei kissed her hard, and she felt a flood of warmth all over as he eased her down on the bed. His hand slid over her sweater and cupped her breast, then rubbed it slowly.

She kissed him back, tangling her tongue with his, sliding her hands over his muscular back. Even with his thick sweater, she could feel Sergei's powerful, hard muscles. The masculinity of his body sent extra thrills zinging inside her as she touched him. His hand moved down and slid under the hem of her sweater, moving back up to caress her breast through the lacy bra.

She became lost in the sensations he evoked. Warmth, longing—the heat of them sped through her.

He paused to pull off her sweater, and bent his head to suckle her nipple through the lace. The erotic pull of his lips sent fire racing through her veins.

She moaned. "Sergei… that feels… so good…"

"Mmm," he murmured, fumbling with the clasp of her bra. He opened it and pulled back for a moment. "You have the most beautiful breasts." He palmed them.

"Kiss them again," she murmured.

"They're perfect." He bent his head and took one bare nipple into his mouth.

She jolted. His mouth was so sensual as he pulled at her, and she moaned again, heat engulfing her down to her very core. She pulled his sweater off and gazed at his hard chest with its sprinkling of black, springy hair. She ran her fingers through it, loving the feel. "Sergei." She stroked his muscles.

He rolled on top of her, somehow ridding himself of his jeans. She helped him unzip and slide her own jeans off.

She was glad she'd worn her sexy, lacy pink bra and matching bikini, which he quickly removed and dropped beside her bed.

He cupped her *there* and she moaned again.

"I want you so much…" he said, kissing her lips.

She couldn't recall ever being so hot, so quickly. "Yes," she said breathlessly. She moved her hand to touch him, through his navy boxer briefs. He was hard as steel.

"Feel what you've done to me?" he whispered huskily, and another thrill went up her spine. She felt powerful.

"Yes," she whispered back, as he continued to play with her, sliding his fingers over her, kissing her breasts. He touched her reverently, at first, then harder.

Then he slid a finger into her wet folds.

"Sergei—I want you—"

He shed his boxers, and producing a condom from his jeans pocket.

All she wanted him to do was plunge inside her.

He slid the condom on. Then he seated himself above her.

"Melissa?"

"Yes," she said, thrusting her hips up.

He dove inside her. He was large, and felt incredibly good.

"Sergei—" was all she could get out, before he began to rock them both.

She felt herself reaching for the summit--

And then suddenly she shattered. "Sergei!"

She was whirling in the sensations that pounded through her. An incredibly intense rush of pleasure!

As she quaked around him, he came with a shout. "Melissa!" His spasms echoed her own.

For a few minutes they held each other. She couldn't think coherently. She just enjoyed the feel of being held by Sergei's strong arms as she floated back to earth.

At some point Sergei shifted their bodies so they were lying side by side, tangled together. Melissa grew almost sleepy with contentment.

She didn't want to fall asleep without offering for him to stay over.

"Sergei…" she whispered.

"That was beautiful," he whispered back. "You are beautiful." He played with a curl of her hair.

She guessed he was feeling as satisfied as her.

"Do you want to stay over tonight?" she murmured.

"I would like nothing better." He didn't hesitate, then kissed her.

She snuggled closer, closing her eyes.

"Just so you know, I only carry one condom in my wallet." He sounded regretful.

"No worries. I have a few in my nightstand drawer. I bought them just 'in case'," she confessed. She opened her eyes to see his reaction.

His smile was wide, his voice husky. "I'm very glad."

She snuggled further into his arms.

***

When Sergei awoke, he was instantly aware of the warm, female body snuggled up to him. Melissa. She had a body which had curves in all the right places.

Sex with her had been amazing. As he held her, skin-to-skin, he felt himself hardening.

She moved against him invitingly.

"Melissa?" He caressed her cheek.

"Yes." Her whisper was throaty.

They made love again, kissing, touching, and he felt incredibly lucky when he slid into her warm body and she clenched around him.

Afterwards they held each other, and once again he drifted into sleep.

When he awoke again, the gray light peeking in the blinds showcased a cloudy morning. He'd slept deeply, satisfied, Melissa's warm body stretched next to him.

He definitely wanted to keep seeing her. This was more than a casual fling. He knew that. He enjoyed her company, and he felt the ultimate satisfaction when she was in his arms.

As he held her, she opened her eyes and smiled, then pressed her body closer and rubbed it against his. "Sergei…" she murmured in a sexy voice.

He kissed her, feeling his dick grow hard instantly.

They made love again. She cried out when she came—twice—and he felt a jolt of masculine pride mixed with pleasure at the sounds.

He came with a shout of satisfaction,

Afterwards, they lay together for a few minutes. He kissed her slowly. "I'd like to take you out to dinner tonight," he suggested.

"That's perfect." She smiled. "Want to take a shower with me?"

He glanced at the clock on her night stand. It was almost 7:30. "Can we do that next time? I have a meeting with my brother and cousin in about an hour. I need to go home and shower there and change into clean clothes." He caressed her face. "I wish I could stay longer."

"Okay."

"How's six o'clock?" he asked, happy that they would spend the evening together.

"That's good," she agreed.

"You decide on a restaurant," he said. She named a popular restaurant a couple of towns over. It was casual but he'd heard the food was really good so he readily agreed.

He rapidly dressed in yesterday's sweater and jeans, then kissed her, lingering over her lips, before leaving. It was one of the most difficult good-byes he'd ever said. He would have loved to remain there with her all day in her bed, with her warm body curled up to his.

***

Wow. What a night.

After her shower, Melissa dressed and dried her hair. She had a quick breakfast while re-living the absolutely hot night she'd spent with Sergei.

She'd known he was a good-looking guy, and had enjoyed the time they'd spent together. But she hadn't expected the blow-your-mind sex. It was extraordinary.

Brad seemed a distant memory at the moment. At least this proved that Brad wasn't the only good lover out there. Was it because it was their first night together?

She thought--she hoped—Sergei had found the sex great too.

Who would have thought that the guy who plowed her parking lot would be the most amazing lover?

It was exactly what she needed, she concluded, sipping her coffee. On impulse she texted Sergei. *Bring clothes for tomorrow. You're invited to sleep over again.*

A minute later, her phone chimed. *Great. I can't wait.*

She finished her coffee, and invigorated, made another cup. While it brewed, she called Rachel and described the date she'd had.

"You were right," Melissa confided. "We had the *most* amazing sex ever. It was exactly what I needed!"

"Yay for you," her friend said. "Are you going to see him again?"

"Tonight, for dinner." She smiled although she knew Rachel couldn't see it. "I'm looking forward to more of the same."

"That's the spirit! You deserve it!"

They chatted for a little while. Then Melissa cleaned the apartment so it would look spotless when Sergei came over.

Since she'd had nothing special planned for the day she relaxed and read, polishing her nails as well. By the time Sergei picked her up she was ready, wearing a nice black skirt and sexy black boots and a clingy sapphire blue top. She made sure she chose another sexy bra and panties set—this time in blue.

And tried not to wait impatiently for Sergei.

CHAPTER VI

Whoa. You going out again, tonight, bro?" Dennis said in the late afternoon, eyeing Sergei.

Dennis had seen him come home this morning, in yesterday's rumpled clothes; but hadn't done anything but raise his eyebrows. Their meeting with Victor had gone smoothly as they reviewed some business plans; and now Sergei was heading out for a night of fun and great sex. With Melissa.

Better yet, she'd invited him to sleep over so they could do it again, and again…

Now Sergei grabbed his coat, eager to get to Melissa's.

"Yes," he answered.

"Who with?"

"It's with whom, jerk," he joked. His grammar had always been better than Dennis'.

Now he silently answered his brother's question. *With a woman I could spend a lot of time with.*

He *hoped* they kept spending time together. He would like a committed relationship. Like Victor had. Like his parents and sister Fania had.

"So whom?"

"Melissa, the girl I was out with last night. "

"The girl whose place you slept at?" Dennis raised his eyebrows.

"Yeah. I'll see you tomorrow."

Dennis gave him a knowing grin.

Sergei thought Dennis might be jealous. He hadn't dated very much lately. Not since he'd hooked up with a girl who lived nearby during the summer, then things hadn't worked out for them for whatever reason.

Once Sergei arrived at Melissa's apartment, they went to the charming restaurant in Mine Hill, which was about half an hour away. It had fine food and a roaring fireplace that made it perfect for a cold winter evening out.

He ordered steak and a loaded baked potato. Melissa ordered the crabcake special with fettuccini. He had red wine, she had white. Despite their different choices of food, it was a relaxing and enjoyable dinner. But there was a certain humming awareness in the air between them, a certain sexual tension that flared like a candle on the Hanukkah menorah. His thoughts drifted to going back to her apartment after dinner and making love.

The thought was very enticing, and he had to tamp down his physical reaction to her. *Down, boy. Spend some time with her. Get to know her better*, he thought. Otherwise, she'll feel like a sex object.

And she wasn't only a sex object. Not to him.

***

"Melissa?" A woman's voice called out to her.

Melissa looked around, then caught sight of a beautiful, dark-haired woman leaving a nearby table. She looked familiar—

She recognized the woman after a second. "Sabrina?"

"Yes. How are you? And—Sergei?" Sabrina continued. A man stood behind her. A hand on her shoulder.

"Hey, Parker; Sabrina." Sergei said, standing to shake the man's hand.

Parker was Melissa's sister Courtney's boss at The Lightning Center, and Sabrina was his wife and the reference librarian there.

That meant Courtney would probably hear about their date, Melissa knew as they spoke with the couple.

Sabrina and Parker had finished eating and were on their way out to the movies, they said. They told Melissa and Sergei to have a nice evening.

Melissa didn't mind Courtney knowing that she was seeing Sergei. She would tell Courtney herself when she spoke to her again. But she hoped her sister didn't mention it to their mother. Mom would demand to know more about the guy she was seeing, and in all likelihood she'd be critical. She had loved Elliott and couldn't understand why Melissa hadn't married him.

Anyway, she and Sergei were simply having fun; they were not in a serious relationship. Her mother never seemed to understand those types of relationships. She would probably disapprove of her adult daughter having a relationship based on sex.

Melissa snapped back to the present. Sergei was asking if she played or liked any sports.

"I'm afraid I'm not very athletic," she admitted. "My mother encouraged me to try tennis, but I didn't care for it. How about you?"

"I like to ski. Dennis and I ski pretty often in the winter. We usually go up to Sussex county, or out to Pennsylvania."

"And Victor too?"

"Not that often. He prefers ice skating. But we all like watching hockey. We've gone to Ranger and New

Jersey Devil games." He grinned. "Would you be interested in going some time?"

A little tingle went up her spine. She wanted to keep seeing him. But she wasn't looking for a long-term relationship, she reminded herself. Still, attending a game would be fun.

"Yes," she answered in a casual voice, "that would be cool." She had gone to a few in-person games with Brad, and found them to be exciting.

"We'll plan a time. Maybe on your Christmas break from school?"

"Sounds like fun."

"Have you ever tried skiing?"

"No. I don't like heights," she answered.

"I could teach you," he offered.

"Mmm… I don't think so." She smiled so he wouldn't take it personally. "I'm too scared."

He didn't push her, which she appreciated. Brad would have kept at her until she agreed to try something. That's how he got her to try golfing. She'd been all thumbs and hated it. And Brad had accused her of "not taking the game seriously."

Forget about your stupid ex, she admonished herself.

She and Sergei went on to discuss other things they liked. She enjoyed singing and had been active in chorus all through school. He told her he and his family did some volunteer work translating for new immigrants in the area.

"That's admirable," she said.

They talked a little about their college experiences, and their families. By the time their delicious dinner was finished, Melissa was happy to sit beside Sergei while he drove back to her place.

Once inside, she couldn't wait to make love with him. Apparently he felt the same, because once they'd hung up their coats and hats, he drew her into his arms. "I've been looking forward to having you in my arms all day," he said huskily, and kissed her hard.

Desire swirled low in her body, and she wrapped her arms around him. They kissed hungrily, and his tongue danced with hers. When he freed her lips, he said, "Melissa… I want you so much."

"I want you too," she said, feeling her heart pound.

She led him to her bedroom, where they quickly rid themselves of their clothes, tumbling beneath the covers. Sergei made a show of removing a bunch of condoms from his pocket as he pulled off his jeans. "I came totally prepared."

"Do you think that's enough?" she teased.

"We can always buy more tomorrow," he said, and pulled her on top of him.

She stroked his shoulders, then moved down to circle each of his nipples with her tongue. He caressed her breasts, then slid his hand down to cup her. The heat inside her flared hotter.

Their love-making was just as wonderful as the night before. When Melissa reached the peak, she shouted out. Sergei followed seconds later, exclaiming loudly. Back to earth, they snuggled close.

***

Sergei was happy to spend a good part of Sunday in bed with Melissa. They made love slowly, then showered together, ate breakfast together, then went back to bed, where they relaxed and talked while listening to music.

They enjoyed each other in a peaceful way. Being with Melisssa was fun, and she was a real sweetheart. Plus the sex was fantastic. She was so passionate, and quickly learned what turned him on the most. He could get used to this, he thought several times during the afternoon, when she was lying content in his arms.

They talked, too. He learned that she'd grown up on Long Island and only recently moved here to north western New Jersey, living near her best friend from college, who'd recommended these apartments; and closer to her sister Courtney. She liked the slower, less hectic and more peaceful lifestyle around here.

They sent out for Chinese food for dinner.

"What are you doing for Hanukkah?" he asked, scooping up some vegetable fried rice. He'd learned that her family did not keep kosher. Since his family didn't either, they could indulge in a lot of food choices without any restrictions.

"I'm not going home next weekend for Hanukkah." She reached for the container that held sweet and sour shrimp. "I'd spend half my time fighting traffic getting there; then I'd have to fight off all the inquiries from my nosy relatives as to what I was doing out here in the remote 'nowhere of New Jersey'" —she made air quotes— "and I don't want more of that." She shook her head. "Uh-uh. I had enough of that kind of thing at Thanksgiving."

He was appalled. "Spending Hanukkah alone? A holiday without your family? You shouldn't do that!" That was unheard of in his family—to not be present at a family gathering for a holiday.

He voiced the thought that popped into his head. "Why don't you spend the first night of Hanukkah with me and my family? It's next weekend. My parents aren't far away. I'll drive us there."

"You want me at your family celebration?" She looked astonished, her mouth dropping open. She had such an expressive face. He could read the emotions passing on it.

"Sure. It's low-key, nothing fancy. We light the candles and have a buffet dinner. My mother's potato latkes are awesome."

He could see uncertainty flash on Melissa's face now.

Reaching for her hand, he tried to smile persuasively. "It will be fun! Please come."

"I hate to get in the way."

"You won't," he urged, suddenly really wanting her there. "I'd like you to be with me. Why should you be all by herself on a holiday? That would be so depressing." He didn't like the thought of her being all alone. The idea stabbed like an icicle piercing him. The Jewish holidays were all about enjoying your family, in his opinion.

Besides, it would give him a chance to introduce her to his family. Since he wanted to keep seeing her, he knew his family would be anxious to meet her.

"Please come," he added, pressing her hand gently.

The undecided expression remained on her face. "Are you sure your parents won't mind?" Doubt tinged her voice.

"Everyone's welcome. And it will be fun," he repeated. "You'll get to meet my brother and sisters and parents. And my cousin and his family are coming too."

"I'll be an unnecessary extra," she protested. "An outsider."

"No you won't. They'll all be glad you're there." He was positive of that.

She seemed to consider as she regarded him.

"Alright," she said, slowly. "As long as I can bring something."

"I'll find out what my mother needs," he promised.

They didn't mention the holiday again, except when he was putting on his jacket to leave, he promised to call her tomorrow and tell her what to bring for the Hanukkah celebration.

Before he left, he cupped her cheek. "I had the best time with you this weekend," he murmured, and kissed her.

"I did too." She smiled up at him.

"Maybe we can see each other Wednesday?" he asked eagerly. He was certain he wanted to spend more time with this woman, get to know her even better.

"Wednesday sounds fine," she said. "Except if you stay here, I need to go to sleep early on school nights."

"Fine with me. I'm used to waking up early," he told her.

When he left, Sergei felt more satisfied than he'd been in years. It had been a fun--and satisfying--weekend. And sex with Melissa was fantastic!

But he also liked spending time in her company. The hours had flown by.

***

"It was a great weekend," Melissa said to Rachel when they met at Rachel's condo Monday night.

Rachel placed paper plates on the kitchen table as they waited for the dinner to be delivered. "Tell me."

"Well… the sex was fabulous. And Sergei was fun to be with. He's considerate and interesting as a person."

"It sounds like you like him." Her best friend raised

her eyebrows. "I thought you wanted a casual fling, no strings attached."

Melissa nodded. "That's exactly what I want. What's wrong with enjoying his company?"

"Nothing's wrong. You should enjoy your lover's company. But you're a romantic. Don't you still sometimes dream of forever… like the dreams you used to have with Brad? And you've been so excited for me and Aaron and our wedding this summer," Rachel continued. She was referring to her fiancé who was working late today,

Rachel had invited Melissa for a girls' night and they planned to watch one of the Hallmark Hanukkah movies that Rachel had DVR'd over the weekend. But first, they'd eat.

"I used to be a romantic," Melissa admitted. "But life has shown me I'm probably never going to find the right guy." Melissa waved her hand in dismissal. "So I'm not going to waste time looking. Besides, you know how most of my family is. They want me to end up with a doctor like Elliott or someone wealthy like Brad. No, I decided to just be a kind of party girl and have a good time. I know that sounds shallow."

"Are you sure that's what you want?" Rachel asked, furrowing her brow. "You're not really a partier, Melissa. You've always stuck to one guy before. And I thought you wanted marriage, security, and a family."

"You know I don't care about status. It used to annoy me that Brad was always showing off how much he could spend. Elliott wasn't like that; but people were always in awe of his being a doctor. As if he was above the average person. I'm just going to enjoy living as much as possible and not worry about the future. I'm not desperately looking for a husband."

"Everyone should enjoy their life--or make changes so they can—like you did when you moved out here." Rachel smiled at her. "But what if the right guy just falls into your lap?"

Her friend went on. "I found love. And so did your sister Courtney. And your sister Sherry is engaged, too." Rachel leaned forward. "Never say never."

"It's highly unlikely. It hasn't happened to me. Not since Brad. It's never going to happen again--I've accepted that fact." Melissa heard the sad note in her own voice. "I am concentrating on the here and now."

"Okay," Rachel said. "You deserve fun, Meliss. If anyone deserves one hot Hanukkah season, you do! You've been working hard. You made changes in your life. Now have fun and enjoy your hot fling!"

Melissa switched the topic. "I'm not sure about going to Sergei's parents' house for Hanukkah. It makes it look more like we're dating."

"So? You are dating! And you know you could have come to our apartment." Rachel had invited her weeks ago, but Melissa had declined. "My immediate family will be the only ones here, since Aaron's family is in Cleveland and we're seeing them during the holiday break from school. Why should you be alone?" It wasn't the first time Rachel had said that. She sounded like Sergei.

Why was everyone so worried about her being alone? It wouldn't be the end of the world to spend a holiday by herself. She didn't mind. She wasn't one of those people who always needed to be around other people.

"I prefer not to be a fifth wheel," she stated to Rachel.

"You wouldn't be here, or at Sergei's, I'm certain. You're friendly. You would blend right in."

"I'm thinking about calling him and telling him I don't want to come."

"I'm sure that would hurt his feelings," Rachel voiced her opinion. "Some families feel the more, the merrier."

"It could be awkward," Melissa said. "It isn't as if Sergei and I know each other well."

"You know each other well enough to sleep together." Rachel pointed her finger at Melissa.

She had a point there. Melissa sat back. "That's true. And I always enjoy his company. But…"

She felt a pit grow in her stomach. Her thoughts and feelings waffled back and forth. Should she go? Should she cancel?

Why the hell couldn't life be simple?

***

Sergei and Dennis usually went to their parents' for dinner every other Monday, depending on their work and weekend schedules. So on Monday they arrived at their parents' small ranch house in Fairlawn before six o'clock.

His sisters, who had their own apartments weren't there tonight. Fania and her husband were working the late shift at the hospital, and Tatiana had a cold.

They were eating his mother's pot roast with vegetables, which was an old-fashioned dish that was delicious. Sergei was reaching for another helping when he remembered he'd have to tell his Mother about their extra guest for Hanukkah.

"What time do you want everyone over for Hanukkah on Saturday?" he asked.

"Come at four," she answered. "Your aunt and Victor's fiancé are making some appetizers."

"I'm bringing a girlfriend over," he blurted.

"A girlfriend?" His father's eyes widened.

"You have a girlfriend?" His mother asked at the same time, then she lapsed into rapid Russian. "You never told me you had a girlfriend! Who is she? Where did you meet?"

"I knew it." Dennis said smugly, in English. "Victor and I were betting you'd bring her here for Hanukkah. I said you would. I'll have to tell him I won the bet."

Sergei's Russian wasn't as good as his parents' and sisters', since he'd spent all his life here in the USA. Still, he could understand what his parents were saying even if he couldn't speak it as well as they did.

When they weren't home, they always spoke English. "We must learn to live like Americans," his parents always said.

He replied in English now. "It's been a new… development. I invited her to come to Hanukkah, since she had nowhere else to go. You can all meet her. She's very nice."

"She better be, if my son likes her." His mother frowned. "What's her name? What does she do? And how come she has no place to go? Doesn't she have a family?" she probed.

His mother sounded aghast at the thought of no family.

"She does have a family. Most of them live on Long Island. She says she doesn't want to travel all the way there for one day."

"That's ridiculous," his father put in.

Oh shit. Now he'd put Melissa in a bad light. "She

doesn't want to fight the horrible traffic going through the city, and on the main highway out there," he said," and she just saw them for Thanksgiving."

"What kind of girl doesn't want to be close to her family?" his mother scoffed.

"She's really nice," he repeated. "Give her a chance. Maybe there's something she doesn't like about her family." *Maybe they're too inquisitive, like mine.*

He decided to concentrate on the positive. "She's a teacher, like Tatiana. But she teaches fourth grade. And her name is Melissa."

"Is she Jewish?" The questions were coming fast and furious now.

"Yes. Reform, like us." He'd learned that during the weekend he'd spent with her. Reform Judaism was the most modern sect of Judaism. His family considered themselves Reform too.

"How did you meet?" his father asked.

"In an odd way." He described how his plow had hit her car, and she'd come running out, and later he'd noticed the menorah in her window.

"You met her when you hit her car?" His dad sat back abruptly, sounding amused. "That's unique. She must resent that."

Dennis started laughing. "It *does* sound ridiculous, bro!"

"Have you been dating her for long?" his mother demanded. "And what kind of girl goes out with someone who ruined her car?"

"We've gotten together a few times." He knew that was a slight exaggeration, but he wanted to put Melissa in the best light. He really liked her, and wanted his family to like her, too. He wasn't about to say "we're good together in bed" to his parents. "And I didn't ruin her car. She's going to have it fixed during her holiday break from school, and my insurance will pay. I'd say that makes her a tolerant woman."

He paused to consider Melissa's personality for a minute. Despite not seeing each other for long, he liked everything he'd learned about her. He felt comfortable with her, and enjoyed her company. And the sex… He couldn't help smiling.

She could be the one, in fact. That thought reverberated in his brain. Had he finally met the woman of his dreams?

His brain warned him not to get too excited. Look what had happened with Tori.

"She offered to bring food for Hanukkah," Sergei added. "What should I tell her to bring?"

"Can she cook?" his mother snapped. She still looked disgruntled.

"Yes." He hoped. Besides, she could always pick up something at the grocery store.

His mother's mouth thinned into a straight line. "She's already cooking for you?"

"Yes." *And making love with me,* Sergei thought, and couldn't help smiling again.

Dennis grinned and leaned close to Sergei. "You got it bad, bro," he whispered.

Yes, he did.

He hoped she did too.

***

Sergei called Tuesday to chat, and told Melissa she could bring over dessert on Saturday.

60

After they hung up, she called Courtney. "What can I bring? He said to bring dessert."

Melissa knew that Courtney had a high school friend who had come from Russia.

"Well, they like vodka a lot, so bring that instead of wine," Courtney advised. "As for dessert… you make good brownies. Why don't you make those?"

"Good idea. Most people like brownies."

Courtney switched the topic. "The whole family misses you. Mom told me she tried to persuade you again to reconsider coming home for Hanukkah."

"No," Melissa said firmly. "I'm not up for all those questions from Aunt Sheila and Aunt Lil. At Thanksgiving it was constantly 'why are you living all the way *out there in the sticks*?' And 'why don't you get back together with that nice doctor?' I can't take it anymore, Courtney. Maybe in a few decades they'll drop those subjects," she finished, with what she hoped sounded like amusement in her voice.

"Sherry said she heard that Elliott got engaged over the Thanksgiving weekend." In fact, he'd gotten engaged within three months of Melissa ending their relationship, but then had broken up with that woman. So much for his undying love for Melissa, she'd thought at the time. And all she truly felt was relief that he'd gone on to find someone who cared about him. Or perhaps the woman simply wanted to marry a doctor.

Now all she could feel was glad that he'd found love and gotten engaged. "I'm happy for him." She said it firmly.

"But now you have a chance to have a relationship with a guy you care about. You do sound like you like Sergei."

Once Melissa had wished she could find true love. But Brad had been a cheater.

And now she'd knew that it probably would never happen for her. And she accepted the fact.

She responded to her sister. "No. We're just having fun. I like him, of course. But anything more—no. It's not happening."

"If you say so." Courtney sounded skeptical.

***

Wednesday Melissa left school as soon as she finished grading some tests. Once home, she freshened her make-up and changed into comfy jeans and a nice purple sweater. Courtney had given her the sweater last Hanukkah and she knew it looked good on her.

Sergei came over a little after four, when she was putting together a simple meatloaf and baked potatoes. Once everything was in the oven, and she had cleaned her hands, she turned to him.

He slid his hands over her and kissed her thoroughly. "I missed you," he said when he freed her lips. His hands remained firmly on her butt, squeezing her gently.

"Really?" She hadn't expected such enthusiasm. Maybe it was the great sex?

"Really. I really did. How long does everything take to cook?" he asked, pulling her tightly against him.

Yeah, he missed the sex, she told herself. *This is turning into a real hot affair.*

She'd missed him and his warmth, his touch, his kisses too. When he kissed her again, she kissed him back just as hard.

"An hour," she said a minute later, hugging him. He

ignited every molecule in her body when he kissed her like this. "That's enough time," she declared with a smile.

He pulled back and grinned, then swung her up into his arms. He carried her to her bedroom and proceeded to touch her and caress her all over. She grew as hot as the flames on a candle.

She wanted to have him inside of her. Now.

"Please, Sergei. Now," she urged.

"Happy to do so." He rolled on a condom, a wide smile lighting his face, then plunged inside her.

She arched her back, taking him deeper. "Oh—Sergei—oh!" She exploded, clenching around his hard member.

He pumped into her, yelling "Melissa!"

They collapsed together.

Afterwards, they cuddled, then dressed, and he offered to set the table.

"Thanks," she said, directing him as to where everything was.

Dinner was nothing fancy, but he praised her cooking. After cleaning up, they sat around and listened to music, and watched a TV show he suggested. It turned out to be funny. A little before eleven, when she told him it was her bedtime, he didn't object. She'd given herself extra time, because she guessed they'd both want to make love again.

And they did.

In his arms, she marveled about how much she enjoyed being with Sergei. It was on the tip of her tongue to say sex with him was the best; but she held back, wondering if he'd read more into it than she meant. Instead she concentrated on the sensations he evoked.

He asked to spend Friday night and all day Saturday

with her before they headed to his parents' house. He even suggested she come to his house and spend Sunday there.

But Friday the forecast changed. They were expecting more snow on Friday night. Not enough to be a major snowstorm; but enough to be a pain, and necessitate snow plowing. Since it was his turn to oversee the guys, he'd have to be out around midnight, he told her, when the snow started. He had to be sure everyone was plowing and there were no truck troubles.

"After the snow has been cleared it will be very late. I don't want to wake you up at 3 AM, so I'll return home," he told her that afternoon.

Melissa was disappointed she couldn't see him, but perhaps it was for the best, she thought, when she got into bed Friday night. She didn't want him thinking this was a serious type of relationship.

***

When he woke in the early afternoon on Saturday, Sergei couldn't wait to see Melissa. He'd wanted to see her badly the night he was stuck supervising, but Victor and his girlfriend had a commitment, and he'd traded once with Dennis; so it had been his turn.

After eating a big breakfast/lunch he showered and dressed in a sweater and nice jeans, then packed a duffle bag with his clothes for tomorrow in case they spent the night at Melissa's instead of here. He texted Melissa that he was on his way, being sure to put the Hanukkah presents he'd bought for her and his family in his truck where she wouldn't notice them.

He'd spent some time at the mall on Thursday, selecting a gift for her—cute Hanukkah socks. He wanted to show he was thinking of her even when they weren't together. That she was important to him. After all, they were spending a lot of time together and each time he'd had fun and liked her more. He didn't want her to think that their relationship was just about sex—though that was great, he had to admit. No, when he caressed her, he felt more than desire—he felt sparks. Sparks of connection. Caring. Whatever it was he wasn't ready to put into words, but it was there. And he wanted Melissa to know it.

***

Melissa talked less than usual on the way to his parents' house.

"Is something wrong?" Sergei asked.

"No, why?"

"You seem quiet."

"I was just thinking about a student," she said, but knew her voice sounded a little defensive. "He has a lot of problems."

She inclined her head down so he wouldn't see the frown she knew was there. Yeah, she was thinking alright. She sneaked a peek to study him as he drove on the interstate through the darkening afternoon.

Why was she going to this party? She didn't know Sergei's family. Maybe she had seen his cousin or brother around once or twice, but she couldn't recall it.

More to the point, she and Sergei had just started their—fling or whatever you'd call it. They weren't in a serious relationship. They had had some good times. They'd had great sex. It was all fun and games—just enjoying themselves. So why on earth did he want to bring her home to meet his family? He'd said it was because she shouldn't be alone on Hanukkah. Was that the truth? After Brad, she'd found it hard to trust men, even Elliott.

She glanced at Sergei. His profile was really handsome. She'd found herself a very masculine lover. But their relationship was simply superficial, wasn't it? Well, wasn't it? she asked herself.

She was afraid to ask what Sergei thought. Leave well enough alone, she told herself. Don't make a big deal. Enjoy it while it lasts. After all, she didn't want any romantic entanglements. That only led to broken hearts. At least for her.

She better make that clear to him when they got back to her home. She didn't want to lead him on, like she had with Elliott. It would be wrong to do so again.

So she better mention her thoughts after the Hanukkah party.

With that decided, she straightened in her seat. She smiled at Sergei. "Tell me about the people who will be there."

"Don't worry if you can't remember everyone's names," he began. "I know it can be overwhelming. And my family can be loud when everyone gets together."

"I'm pretty good at names," Melissa said. "I have to learn my students' names quickly."

"Well, you'll meet my parents, Arkady and Helena, and my brother Dennis. You've probably seen him around. And my sisters—Tatiana is the teacher, and Fania is a doctor. Fania and her husband got married last year and her husband is coming too, although he gets emergency calls often. He's a pediatrician."

"What kind of doctor is Fania?"

"A kidney specialist."

She nodded.

"Then there's my cousin Victor," Sergei continued, "and his fiancé, Abby. She's not Jewish so we'll be explaining some of the customs to her. And Victor's sister, my cousin Lara. She has a new boyfriend so you won't be the only stranger there."

"It will be easier for me to remember them after I actually meet them." There were going to be more people there than she had expected. The fact that at least one other person was a stranger was reassuring.

"Oh, and my dad's cousin Leo, who never married. My parents don't want him to feel alone on a holiday."

So that's why he had invited her. He'd been telling the truth. His family was used to doing that. It made complete sense now.

Feeling more comfortable, she sat back. She was just being included since Sergei's family couldn't bear the idea of people being alone on holidays, even minor ones on the Jewish calendar. She felt better knowing that. It wasn't as if his bringing her indicated they were in some kind of relationship or anything.

She glanced down at the shiny blue, festive bag in which she'd placed a bottle of expensive vodka. Beside it, on the truck's floor, she'd wrapped some fancy Hanukkah chocolates she'd found in a candy store.

She relaxed into the comfy seat of his blue truck.

She asked him a couple of questions about his family members as they drove through the darkening afternoon. Melissa recognized some of the towns they drove through on Interstate 80, because Courtney and Ben lived not far from their destination.

Sergei pulled up in a neighborhood of smaller

homes, mostly ranches, cape-cods and bilevels. Probably built in the late 40s and early 50s, she guessed. The homes looked a little older than the neighborhood in which she'd grown up on Long Island.

There were cars and a few trucks crowding the driveway, and spilling onto the street. The house that he led her to was a white ranch with a single garage, and a wide window displaying Hanukkah decorations. Lights were on and the noise of people chattering reached her as Sergei opened the door. Delicious aromas teased her nose.

Her first impression was that the home was warm and festive. The furniture was simple and included a mix of decorative items—some old, like an old-fashioned vase full of colorful flowers, and some new, like the large Wide-screen TV.

"Hey bro." A man who looked strikingly like Sergei stepped up to them. Sergei introduced his brother, Dennis to her and they shook hands.

After that she was introduced to a dizzying array of people. Some older, like Sergei's parents and some younger, like his cousin Victor, who had a strong resemblance to Sergei and Dennis. In fact the Rubenov men all looked a lot alike, she observed.

Sergei's mother studied her, then when Melissa handed over the Vodka and candy, hugged her. "Thank you. We'll open these later. It's so nice to meet you, Melissa." Her accented voice was friendly.

"Yes, we're glad to meet you. We've heard so much about you. You are a teacher, yes?" said Sergei's father.

Before she could say much, Sergei was introducing his aunt and uncle, and his dad's cousin, whom he called "uncle."

She strove to remember all the names as they wound

through the living room and dining room, all packed with jovial people.

"I hope I remember everyone's names," Melissa murmured to Victor's girlfriend Abby.

"You will," Abby told her, smiling. She was a tall blonde and very attractive. "It took me a while, the first time I met everyone. Of course, I know Dennis and Sergei best cause I saw them around at the house. You know—the home they all shared when they lived together. Now that Victor moved in with me, we're planning to buy a house at some point, so Sergei and Dennis are buying out his share."

That was news to her, but of course Sergei didn't share everything about his life, Melissa realized. And neither did she.

"How long have you known Victor?" she asked Abby.

"About two years. We met at a party one of his friends had. My roommate and I lived across the hall in our apartment building and his friend invited us to the party." She was very talkative, Melissa observed. But she didn't mind. It saved her from meeting everyone at the same time.

Sergei's cousin Lara had introduced her boyfriend Alex. When he went to get a soda, she sidled up to Melissa. "A lot of people to meet at once, huh?" she asked.

"Yeah. I hope I remember all the names," Melissa joked.

"Yeah. I hope Alex makes a good impression," she said. "I guess you want to too?"

That surprised Melissa. "I haven't really worried about it," she said frankly. "I haven't known Sergei for too long and it was a last-minute decision to bring me."

"Oh, it's a little different for Alex and me. I think I'm falling for him and I want everyone to like him," Lara confessed in a serious voice.

Melissa just smiled. What was there to say? That she wasn't worried about a long-term thing?

Then she caught Sergei looking at her. He'd been talking to Victor and Victor's dad across the room. But the slow smile he gave her warmed her inside.

This shouldn't be happening, she scolded herself silently. *You shouldn't feel this warmth curling inside of you. You're just having a holiday fling. A fun affair. One hot Hanukkah, right?*

Right!

Her reaction must be because of the warmth of Sergei's family and all the happiness of a holiday, Melissa decided.

Nothing else.

"Want something to drink?" Sergei sidled up to her.

Yes, thanks." A cold drink would be a good idea. "Just soda."

When Sergei returned two women and one man were with him. He introduced his sisters and Fania's husband. The sisters both had dark hair and looked alike, but one—Fania—was taller.

"Have some." Sergei's aunt was passing around a charcuterie board with a variety of cheese and crackers, dried fruit and nuts.

His aunt began to pepper Melissa with questions. Where did she live? How long had she been seeing Sergei? And did she have brothers and sisters?

As soon as she answered one question, his aunt would ask another. Melissa felt relief when she went to pass around the appetizers to others.

Tatiana and Fania had questions too. How had she met Sergei? They laughed when Sergei described the accident, but looked sympathetic when learning that Melissa taught fourth grade.

"The little ones are difficult to teach." Tatiana had a trace of an accent, not as heavy as her parents'. "I prefer the older ones."

"But they're harder to motivate," Melissa said.

"That's true. But I get a lot of smart students in my chemistry classes. The ones who are less interested in doing well in school take easier subjects."

Melissa and Sergei moved around the house, talking to different family members. Then Sergei's mother and aunt and sisters laid out the dinner, buffet-style. There was brisket; and the traditional potato latkes with a choice of applesauce or sour cream; and carrots with a glaze and a green bean dish. Plus a dish she was told was pishka, a traditional Russian vegetable dish of sauteed mushrooms and onions. There was also a salad including beets. Everything smelled tempting. She wanted to try a little of each.

She noticed Sergei and his brother and cousin took generous portions of everything. "We have more in the kitchen," his mother declared.

She spotted a Challah, the traditional yeast bread in a braided shape. She pointed at it. "That looks good."

"It's home made," Sergei said proudly. "My aunt and cousin have been experimenting with baking their own bread."

The food *was* delicious. Melissa complimented everyone who'd worked on the meal. She was glad she'd contributed to the desserts. Sergei had brought in her platter of brownies when he brought in his bag full of gifts for his siblings.

They ate, and the younger people joked around, mostly in English, but with an occasional phrase in Russian, which Sergei would translate for her. Melissa felt the tension slip from her body as they included her in conversations as if she was an old friend.

They watched while Sergei's mother lit the Hanukkah menorah when darkness fell outside. Everyone recited the traditional blessing. Sergei's dad told a very shortened version of the story of Hanukkah for Abby's benefit.

"Today we celebrate the fact that the first temple, which was destroyed by the Assyrians, was cleaned up and made whole by our people. They discovered oil for the Eternal Light; but thought it would only last for one night. But then a miracle occurred—and the oil lasted for eight nights and days, until new oil could be found. And that is why the Jewish people celebrate Hanukkah, the festival of lights, for eight nights."

"Good description, dad," Dennis called out. "You kept it short."

People chuckled, and started helping themselves to the desserts.

Besides her brownies, there was a vanilla and chocolate bundt cake; a whole bunch of the traditional fried jelly doughnuts; and some assorted cookies. Melissa chose a brownie and a jelly doughnut. She was already getting full.

"These brownies are good," Victor said, chewing on one.

"She's a good cook besides being a good baker," Sergei bragged, and Melissa felt her cheeks flush.

"Thanks," she mumbled.

"Don't be modest. You are a good cook, and baker." Sergei reached for another brownie.

"Are you Reform or Conservative?" Sergei's aunt asked. "I'm guessing Sergei would have mentioned if you were Orthodox and warned us to keep the meal Kosher."

"Yes, I'm Reform," Melissa said.

His aunt must be very nosy, she concluded as the woman barraged her with more questions. Where did she live? She said she could hear her New York accent. Where had she attended college?

"Actually, I lived most of my life on Long Island," Melissa said.

"I see."

When she asked her "Where did your people come from originally?" Sergei stepped in to rescue her.

"Let's give Melissa a break from all the questions," he chided. "She just met everyone. I don't want her to think everyone's giving her a hard time." His mouth set in a straight line.

"Let's open the gifts!" Victor suggested. It sounded like he felt sympathy for her, Melissa realized.

His sister agreed loudly "Good idea!"

Gifts were soon being distributed. Melissa was glad that Sergei's dad seemed happy with her choice of vodka.

Fania handed her a gift. "For you."

Astonished, she looked at Sergei's sister. "For me?"

"It's from *all* of us." Fania gave a little laugh. "Just something small."

Melissa opened the small gold gift bag. Inside was an Amazon gift card for twenty-five dollars.

"Thank you everyone!" Melissa said loudly, so she could be heard over the din. People were exclaiming and tearing paper wrap. "I wanted to buy a couple of books. This will be perfect."

"You like to read?" Fania asked.

"I love reading," she confirmed.

She sat back to enjoy watching the others open their gifts. Fania had gotten a beautiful blue sweater from her sister, and Tatiana a small Coach designer purse from Fania, she noticed.

Dennis had given Sergei a nice navy blue sweater, and he got some other nice gifts, too.

Sergei's mother seemed to like the chocolates Melissa had brought, and she felt embarrassed that she hadn't been more prepared for the party with additional gifts.

She felt her cheeks flush further when Sergei handed her a small blue gift bag.

"For you," he said, his voice low.

"For me? But—but I didn't bring anything for you." This was a shock. She felt a stab of guilt.

Her mind scrambled. Could she give him a late gift this week? She hadn't expected anything from him. Not after seeing each other for only a few weeks! Elliott had certainly not given her anything for several months. And Brad—well, he had always shown off, but his gifts were more about impressing everyone around, like giving her an expensive perfume or a designer handbag which she could show off to their mutual friends.

She took the bag gingerly from Sergei's hands.

She pulled out a soft pair of socks with a design of gold dreidels and menorahs on it. Hanukkah socks!

"Oh, these are cute! And so soft." She smoothed her fingers over them.

"I noticed you like to wear socks around the house," he said.

"I do. I never liked wearing shoes inside," she said. "I'm sure these will be comfortable."

"I'm glad you like it," he said simply.

Her hands began shaking. *He wanted to find something cute for her. And he had noticed she liked wearing just socks at home.*

She looked back at him. He was smiling softly.

She should be very grateful. She went to kiss him gently on the cheek, conscious that some of his relations were watching, especially his nosy aunt and his mom. "Thank you," she murmured in his ear. "You're very thoughtful."

But inside she felt torn. She had come here reluctantly, and now Sergei was giving her a gift—an inexpensive one, but still a gift. *This could give a whole new meaning to their relationship. A meaning she hadn't expected—or wanted.*

Their relationship was supposed to be about having fun, booty calls and a hot Hanukkah season.

But Sergei seemed to have other ideas.

CHAPTER VII

Melissa's fingers had trembled when she opened his gift.

What did that mean? Sergei wondered. Was she nervous for some reason? Did she not like opening gifts?

He noticed a flush creep up her neck and face. She appeared almost—embarrassed, he decided.

Oh he got it. She was embarrassed since she hadn't brought him a gift.

"Sergei, I—I—" she stopped.

"It's alright," he whispered. "I understand you didn't… expect anything. But I wanted to give you something." He smiled at her flushed face.

Then he became conscious of several pairs of eyes on them amidst the cheerful people in the room.

"Nice, bro," Dennis said from close to his shoulder.

"You have good taste," Fania added. "I love those socks. I want a pair," she joked.

Meanwhile, Melissa's cheeks had grown increasingly rosy, and her expressive face looked uncertain.

"I think I'll get more soda," she said abruptly, and headed for the kitchen.

A pang struck his stomach. He'd put some thought into the gift. He'd tucked something more expensive into his truck to give her later, when they were alone. But in front of the family didn't seem like the right time to give it to her.

But he'd genuinely wanted to give her something special. The socks hadn't been expensive. He wanted to spend money on her, but didn't want to go overboard. He *liked* Melissa. A lot. And he wanted to show her that.

He hadn't expected her to get embarrassed. He knew his feelings were rapidly growing. She just might be the girl of his dreams. He'd been thinking that thought for days.

Had he been too pushy? Had he made assumptions?

He followed her into the kitchen.

"Melissa—" he said as he stood next to her.

She gave him a wavering smile. "Thank you Sergei. It's very thoughtful of you to get me something. But I didn't expect it. I don't have anything for you."

"That's alright," he said in a reassuring voice.

"Let's—let's talk about this later." She smiled again, briefly, then went to join the rest of his family.

What had he done wrong? Was he coming on too strong?

***

Oy, was all Melissa could think.

She had never expected that Sergei would get her a present.

She knew it was thoughtful of him. But it implied things that couldn't be between the two of them.

They needed to talk, to get things out in the open. Their expectations and realities for this relationship needed discussion.

She thought that she had made it clear that she was not looking for a serious relationship. Now she was worried that she hadn't. She had ended things too late with Elliott, and she had crushed him. It had been cruel of her.

It was better to get control of the situation in the beginning so Sergei wouldn't develop feelings for her—feelings she could not return.

She had to make it clear what *her* intentions were.

Maybe they should leave early. But she didn't want to insult Sergei's family.

Fortunately, twenty minutes later Fania announced she had early morning rounds to do on patients in the hospital, and she and her husband had to leave. They started their good-byes.

Victor and Abby followed.

Melissa gave Sergei a look that she hoped he'd interpret as "let's go too."

He did. He walked up to her and asked in a low voice if she was ready to leave. She nodded.

They started leaving, which took a good fifteen minutes, between saying goodbye to everyone, thanking them for the gifts, and receiving some leftovers, which Sergei's Mom insisted they take. Unfortunately, there were no latkes left. It was no wonder, Melissa thought. They'd been delicious.

They were mostly quiet on the drive back. She suggested going to her apartment first, before his home. If they had a disagreement over what she had to say, it might be better if she stayed at her place.

I better let him know that his family was nice.

"I like your family," she began. "They're very nice."

"They liked you too. A lot. I could tell."

Oy, that made it worse. She wasn't looking to impress them.

Once they arrived at her apartment, they went inside. "Can we talk for a few minutes?" she asked.

They had removed their coats and hats, and put the leftovers in her fridge. They sat on her couch.

"I feel bad that I didn't get you a gift and you got me one," she said as soon as they sat down. "It was unnecessary. I'm—embarrassed." She regarded him.

"Don't be." He shifted his position. "I like you, Melissa, and wanted to get you something."

"It was more than that." She didn't beat around the bush. "Sergei, I thought we were only casually dating! I didn't expect a gift at all."

He appeared confused. "Well, yes, we started with casually dating. But I like you a lot."

She shook her head. "Maybe I should tell you about my past. Then you won't—" she paused— "take this relationship too seriously." She really didn't want to hurt him.

"Maybe you should, and I'll share mine." Now he looked determined.

She took a deep breath. "Near the end of my college years, I met Brad. He was handsome and thoughtful and everything I thought I wanted in a guy." She pictured the man who'd broken her heart. Brad had been tall, blond, attractive—and with a swagger in his step.

She didn't mention that. "I was totally in love," she admitted. "And I thought he was too."

"What happened?"

"We dated for almost two years. I was sure he was about to propose. We saw each other most weekends and sometimes during the week. One evening I decided to surprise him at his apartment with the news that I'd gotten a good teaching job, not far from where he grew up. I went over to his apartment—and walked in on him making love to another woman on his couch." She swallowed, her throat growing thick. "I couldn't believe it. It turned out he'd been dating her for a while. Her family had influence and money. It came out that he thought they could—advance his career. *She* thought they were about to get engaged too."

"That's terrible." He reached for her hand, but she pulled it away and clasped it with her own. "Anyway, I broke up with him immediately," she continued. "But I was totally devastated."

"It's not surprising," Sergei declared.

"I was not interested in dating for months after that. My family kept trying to fix me up." She took a deep breath. "Then I met Elliott. He was a doctor, and everyone assumed I would settle down with him."

Sergei's eyebrows rose. His mouth set in a line.

"But I never had more than a liking for him. We had some good times, and it was a comfortable relationship. After almost two years, when my sister Courtney was getting together with Ben, I realized that I didn't have strong feelings for Elliott. I could see the difference between my feelings and Courtney's. And it was terribly unfair for me to string Elliott along when he could be finding a woman who truly loved him. He was a nice guy. He deserved to find the right woman. But that woman wasn't me! So I broke up with him."

"And…" he leaned closer.

"I wasn't sorry. He did eventually meet someone. I heard recently that he's engaged, I'm happy for him," she concluded.

"So what's the problem?" He waved one hand.

"I realized my life will be different than most women's. I can never love anyone the way I loved Brad. I can't risk it, risk the hurt. And I won't string someone along the way I did with Elliott. It's just plain wrong."

She paused and drew a sharp breath. "I'm just destined to spend my life alone, and I'll try and make the best of it." Why was her throat closing up? She had accepted her fate.

"I see."

He stared at her, but his expression remained closed-off. Unreadable, at least to her.

"So… what happened to you?" she questioned.

"I met Tori three years ago, at a Bar Mitzvah for one of my cousins. His family was close friends of hers. She was attractive and lively and we had a good time together. We began dating and I fell in love with her." He paused.

"And?" she prodded.

"She wanted to see my family often. I thought that was a good thing. She seemed to want to get close to my mother. It seemed like she was kissing up to her and I started getting annoyed. I found out she had an ulterior motive." His mouth tightened visibly.

"She had majored in art and was a salesclerk at a crafts store, but she was trying to start her career as an artist. A painter. She thought my mother's connections would help her career. That's why she kept trying to hang around with her. That's why she was dating me."

"Oh! That's awful!"

He flushed. "I rarely talk about my mother's job. She conducts tours in Russian, for Russian-speaking tourists at some important museums in New York City including several very famous art museums. Tori thought, mistakenly, that my mother had connections in the art world. She doesn't."

His face darkened as he went on. "I felt used. That's when I broke it off." Anger vibrated in his voice now.

"That's terrible," Melissa said. "She sounds like a

witch." Melissa felt her stomach twist in sympathy with Sergei. She wanted to use another word, a harsher one that started with a "b" but she refrained. He obviously caught her meaning. His eyes met hers.

Although she felt bad for him, she felt a little relief too. "I can see why you wouldn't want to get involved." *We can just enjoy a hot holiday.*

"That's just it." He shook his head. "I do want to get involved—with *you*, Melissa."

CHAPTER VIII

What? Melissa's mouth dropped open. "But—but Sergei, I've been through the same thing as you. Or almost. My cheating boyfriend was a horrible betrayal. I don't want to get involved."

He reached out and stroked her cheek softly. She shivered. *It's just desire, silly,* she told herself.

"I understand that," he said, his words soft. "But, you can trust me. I want you to trust me. I think we could have something special."

"No—I—" her thoughts whirled.

He pulled her into his arms and kissed her. Her thoughts flew out the window.

She opened her mouth automatically and his tongue thrust inside, tasting of brownies and coffee. Their tongues danced together and she felt the familiar heat low in her body. It spread rapidly into a conflagration, and she locked her arms around his neck.

He pulled away. "Give me a chance to convince you." His kisses switched from incendiary to tender. "I believe we would be great together. I'm laying it on the line with you, Melissa. Believe me."

She pulled back to stare at Sergei. His words cooled her passion.

"You—"

"I want a chance," he said, taking her hand in his and kissing it.

"But—but we're just having fun," she protested. "We're just having one hot Hanukkah which we can enjoy together. You need it as much as I do!"

"It's more than that," he insisted. "I think we can have more than one Hanukkah together." He kissed her hard. "And you can trust me. I won't cheat." His voice rang with reassurance.

Could she? "I thought I could trust Brad." Her voice was low. "But I shouldn't have."

"I'm not Brad." His mouth tightened. "Not even close. He was a bastard."

They sat silently for a minute. She wondered, could she trust Sergei? So far he'd given her no reason to distrust him. But—experience had taught her you couldn't trust most guys. Except for Courtney's husband Ben. And Rachel's fiancé Aaron. Those were some good men, she reminded herself. So maybe…

No, one half of her protested. *You've decided you will go through life without a commitment.*

Trust him, the other half said.

She felt, almost physically, the push--pull of two opposite feelings.

She stared at Sergei.

"Please, take the chance on me," he whispered.

"I don't know…" she usually wasn't so conflicted. "I thought we were in this for fun."

He kissed her, gently this time. "I want more than sex, Melissa. And I'll prove it."

"How?" she nearly scoffed.

"Let's see each other for a while. Simply date. No strings attached. And unless you ask, we won't make love."

"Go without sex?" Her voice came out shaky. She felt stunned. Their sexual relationship was so good… why give it up?

"Yes, unless you tell me you want it. I'll prove that I care for you for more than one hot Hanukkah," he repeated her words, making them sound almost amusing.

She leaned back to regard him.

Despite her misgivings, it sounded quite logical. Either their relationship would continue, and they would go back to having hot sex, or if it turned out the affair was no good, they could part ways. Relief began to flood her veins. There would be no pressure from him. They could enjoy each other's company without her being more involved. And when (and if) she agreed, each other's bodies. Which she definitely wanted in the future, even if she didn't want more.

"I agree," she said. "But… Sergei, I want to go to bed with you… now." He had gotten her all hot before, and she still wanted him. To prove it, she pulled him close to her and kissed him hard.

"Are you sure, Melissa? I really want to prove my feelings are more than just plain desire."

"Yes." She practically climbed onto his lap.

Sex was, as usual, wonderful. Was she imagining it, she wondered, or did Sergei take special care to see that she got lots of pleasure? It seemed that he caressed her more sweetly, and concentrated even more than usual on bringing her to the peak—more than once. He was a wonderful lover, she thought hazily as he brought her extraordinary pleasure again.

Afterwards, Sergei insisted on going home for the night, to prove he wasn't using her. But he invited her to his house for the second night of Hanukkah. He asked her to come to his home tomorrow and share the leftovers, which he took out of her fridge.

Alone, after putting on her old flannel pjs, Melissa pondered what he'd said. She came to no conclusions about their relationship. The sex was great, but if he expected more… she hated to disappoint him. He was so nice.

And the thought that they could actually be a couple—well, that was highly unlikely. She couldn't believe the idea.

Was she just using Sergei for fun? That idea was incredibly selfish. Yet he seemed to enjoy the sex as much as she did.

She tossed and turned before dropping into a troubled sleep.

***

When Sergei awoke the next morning and stumbled to the kitchen to get coffee, Dennis was already up.

"What's wrong? I noticed your truck when I woke up," his brother said. "Have an argument with your girlfriend?"

"In a way." Coffee in hand, Sergei sat down across the living room from Dennis and spilled out his story. Dennis currently had no steady girlfriend, but he had dated quite a few women.

"Well, bro, you could just go along with it, and have a lot of sex," Dennis said. "Like she said one hot Hanukkah. Enjoy it!"

Sergei frowned. "But I want more. I really care about her."

"But she may never feel the same."

Sergei shook his head. "I have to try. I have to take a chance that her feelings will grow."

"I don't want to see you get hurt in the process," his brother said.

"I won't." He knew his voice sounded grim. "In the meantime, she's coming here for dinner. I've gotta straighten up this place. We have some leftovers from yesterday. Want to join us for supper?"

"No, thanks. I'll stay out of the way." His brother shook his head. "I don't want to be accused of interfering."

After breakfast, Sergei unpacked his duffle bag. He found the silver bracelet he'd had inside, all wrapped up in shiny silver paper. He'd intended to give it to Melissa, but decided to wait for a more intimate moment, not in front of his family. But once they'd had their discussion, he'd forgotten about it. He was getting as absent-minded as Dennis, he scolded himself.

***

"It sounds like he's crazy about you," Rachel said on the phone when Melissa awoke and called her.

Melissa had called her while sipping her second cup of coffee. Melissa desperately wanted the advice of her closest friend.

"So what's the problem?" Rachel continued as Melissa was silent.

"I don't want him to fall for me. I don't want to be in the same situation I was in with Elliott."

"You mean dating a guy who cared more than you did?"

"Yes. With Elliott I felt constantly guilty after a few

months. I knew it would never amount to anything. I was guilty of stringing him along because it was comfortable."

"And you think the same will happen with you and Sergei," Rachel stated.

"Yes. I'll never love anyone like I did Brad," Melissa said.

"How do you know that?" Rachel challenged. "If you give yourself a chance, you might find love again. With someone trustworthy this time," she added.

Melissa shook her head automatically, though Rachel couldn't see her. "It's never going to happen."

"Don't be too sure," Rachel warned. She began to hum.

Melissa remembered, how, in college, Rachel had been dumped by a boyfriend and been heartbroken. For weeks she went around singing "I'll Never Fall in Love Again" because she grew up listening to her mother playing her collection of Broadway albums. The song was a famous song from "Promises, Promises."

Now Melissa recognized the tune.

"I won't fall in love again," she insisted to Rachel.

This should be my anthem, Melissa thought. She was not about to fall in love. She was never going to make that mistake again.

***

Sergei texted her later that morning asking if she could bring frozen latkes or something like that to add to their dinner, since there had been none left over the night before.

She knew a specialty market that would probably have them, so she called and reserved an order of sixteen, knowing they'd each have some leftovers from the batch. She texted him back afterwards, then decided to call Courtney.

Her sister greeted her enthusiastically. "Hi Melissa! What's going on?"

Melissa sighed, poured out her conflicted feelings and Sergei's declaration that he wanted to get closer, and his history with Tori. "I told him about Brad, and Elliott. I also told him," she finished, "that I will never fall in love again."

"What?" her sister exclaimed. "You said that to him?"

"Yes. It's the truth!" Why did she feel like she had to defend herself, first with her best friend, then with her sister? "But you know all this," she added. "It's nothing new."

"But Meliss, you should never say it can't happen. My boss Meredith thought the same thing, but you've met her, and her husband. She fell in love with him even though she never expected to. Sometimes it just happens. It's fate. Look at Ben, and me."

Melissa knew Courtney believed Ben had been her true love in a past life. "But it doesn't happen to everyone," she argued. "I don't believe it will ever happen to me. I met my love, and Brad betrayed me."

Courtney scoffed. "It doesn't mean it can't happen again. Don't close yourself off. If you give him a chance, it could happen," she urged. "Why don't you give him that opportunity? He's a good guy, Melissa. It sounds like he really *is* into you. He might be the one to break through that shell you're creating around yourself to keep from being hurt again. Grab the opportunity!"

"I was devastated after Brad. You *know* that! I never

want to go through that again," Melissa insisted. "I don't think I ever recovered, Courtney. Even now."

"So you're going to avoid love for your whole life? That means you could end up alone… and regretful," her sister pointed out.

"I've accepted it," Melissa stated.

But inside, she wondered… could Courtney possibly be right? Her sister was often wise about things. She claimed it was the accumulated knowledge from past lives. Melissa believed it was possible. But… did it apply to *her*?

"Just… give him a chance," Courtney advised. "Keep seeing him, and see what happens."

She didn't agree. "I could get hurt all over again."

"That's part of life," Courtney said. "There are no guarantees. Even if you wall yourself off, Melissa, things happen. A student could get hurt. Your principal goes bananas. Someone drops you as a friend. You can get hurt by a lot of things. You can't stop living, you know."

"I know. But…" Melissa sighed. "You sound like Mom."

"Listen, I know what I'm talking about. Ask Rachel. I know about the guy who dumped her. Now she'd engaged to a great guy. And my boss Meredith is married and very happy."

"I'll think about it." That was all she would reluctantly promise.

"I hate to think of you isolated and avoiding all the fun involved in life and love." Courtney sounded sad.

Melissa murmured something non-committal. "We'll see."

"Think about what I said, okay?" her sister urged.

When they disconnected, Courtney's advice barreled

through Melissa's brain. Her thoughts bounced around. Could her sister be right? Was she avoiding life?

***

Melissa arrived promptly at Sergei's home. It was easy to find, on a side street in a hilly area. She could see it was a well-maintained ranch that was larger than some of the other homes nearby.

She parked in the large, expanded driveway, recognizing Sergei's blue truck. She took out the boxed chocolate cake she'd bought at the marketplace nearby, and the latkes. She hadn't brought her duffle because even if this turned out to be another booty call, she had no intention of sleeping over. Like Sergei, she didn't want tonight to be too intimate. Besides, she'd have to be up early for school tomorrow.

She didn't see Dennis' truck as she walked to the front door. Was he making himself scarce?

She knocked on the door. Sergei opened it, smiling broadly. "Melissa." He pulled her into his arms and gave her a loud, smacking kiss. "I'm happy you're here."

"Me too." She couldn't help the warmth spreading through her. *It's just sexual heat,* she told herself. Firmly.

"I'll heat up the brisket now," Sergei said. "And I made a salad."

He led her to a large kitchen, which must have been modernized at some point recently. The stainless appliances and white cabinets looked new, and there was a large black and white granite counter.

She handed him the latkes and placed the cake in its box on the counter.

He took out a salad and then put the leftover brisket

in the microwave to heat up. "Where's Dennis?" she asked.

"He went to a friend's house. We get to be alone for a while." He waggled his eyebrows. "Let's light the candles."

They lit the main candle--the shamash, and the two candles for the second night. They chanted the traditional prayer together, his deeper voice combining with hers. He reached for her hand and held it while they said the prayer.

Sweet, she thought. Then: *no, no, no. Don't get too comfortable.*

His modern silver-toned Hanukkah menorah stood on a decorative platter that said "Happy Hanukkah!" After they chanted the prayer, she asked him where he'd gotten the platter to hold the menorah. She hadn't seen one like it before.

"My mom bought one for each of us kids when she got hers," he explained.

"I just keep mine on a large piece of aluminum foil," she admitted. "But it doesn't look as nice as this. And the candles always drip so I need something."

"Mine always do too."

The dinner was delicious. The brisket was still tasty, even when re-warmed; and the latkes from the specialty store tasted almost as good as home-made. Melissa had brought applesauce to put on top. Sergei preferred sour cream, which he had in his refrigerator, so he added that. They chatted about Hanukkah traditions in each other's families. As they were finishing dinner his cellphone interrupted.

"It's Dennis." He looked at it and frowned. "I'll see what he wants." He answered, then listened.

He looked at Melissa.

He said something in Russian that sounded like it might be a curse.

"What is it?" She leaned towards him.

He said something else to his brother, and hung up. "One of the guys is having trouble with a plow we had serviced recently. Something's not right. We have to go over and check it out. I'm the best at fixing these things." It was a simple statement, not a boastful one.

"I understand," she said. "How long will you be gone? I can go home now." Although she really didn't want to—she was enjoying herself.

"About forty-five minutes, if we can fix it right away. Please stay, Melissa." He touched her hand lightly. "We're supposed to get snow tomorrow night so they want me to look at it now, in case I have to get a part tomorrow." He grimaced. "This interrupts our time together. I'm sorry."

He sighed and began clearing the table. "Our trucks are parked in the industrial complex where we have our office. It's only a few minutes from here."

"I'll help clean up dinner." She stood, and gathered up some utensils. "And I'll stay here until you get back."

He flashed her a smile. "Thank you. I want to spend more time with you. Oh, we have sandwich bags for the leftover latkes." He pulled them out of a drawer. "Feel free to turn on the TV." He waved at the living room area.

"I'll see you soon," she told him as he dashed to the closet, pulling out his coat and muttering in Russian.

"See you soon!" he called, and left.

She cleared the rest of the table. Then she rinsed off the dishes and stacked them in the expensive-looking dishwasher.

She pulled out her cellphone, looking at the time. It

was still early, not quite 7:30. She walked into the living/family room space, figuring she'd turn on the large TV and flip around to see if there were any interesting programs on.

She settled in front of the TV, feeling a curious gap. She missed Sergei's presence.

She was watching a competitive cooking show when the doorbell rang.

She started. Who could that be? Sergei hadn't said he was expecting anyone. He or Dennis wouldn't ring the bell—they'd simply use their keys. Maybe a delivery driver?

She got up and started towards the door.

Approaching it, she stood on tiptoes to see out the peephole.

A blonde woman in a stylish red coat stood outside.

"Who's there?" Melissa called out.

"It's me."

"Who?" she asked in a louder voice.

"I'm here to see Sergei and Dennis." Her voice was strident. "It's Tori. Let me in."

CHAPTER IX

T*ori?*

Shock reverberated through Melissa. Stunned, she stepped back.

"Are you one of their friends?" Tori shouted. "It's cold out here. Let me in!"

"No!" She was not letting some strange woman inside Sergei and Dennis' home. What if she was an axe murderer or something equally terrible? Scenes from TV crime shows played in Melissa's mind.

"What do you mean no?" Tori exclaimed. She hammered on the door. "Let me in, damn it!"

"No!" Melissa yelled back. "I don't know you. You can wait in your car til the guys get back."

"They'll be livid!" Tori pounded on the door again.

"I don't care. I'm not opening this door! And," Melissa shouted just as loudly, "if you don't stop pounding on it, I'm calling the police!"

"The police!" But she stopped her hammering. "Sergei will be so mad at you."

"I'm his girlfriend." Melissa retorted. *Kind of.*

Complete silence followed Melissa's statement.

A minute later, Tori began yelling again. "What the hell do you mean? *Where's Sergei and Dennis?* I demand to come inside.*"

"Absolutely not!" Melissa snapped back. She thought of serial killers on the news and stepped back.

"I was invited to come here." The snarl in the woman's voice seemed to echo. Then Melissa heard her stomp off.

She ran to the front window of the living room and peeked out, trying to remain hidden from view. Sure enough, the woman in the red coat—who had probably bleached her hair—had whirled back to a fancy-looking black car.

As Melissa stared, trying not to be seen, the woman opened the car, slid in, and slammed the door shut. The engine started, and she sat there, not moving the car.

Melissa ducked back to the kitchen and paced.

She was not about to let in this stranger. But… why did she insist she was there to see Sergei and Dennis? Sergei had said he'd broken up with her. *What the hell was going on?*

Her steps slowed. Had Sergei lied? A chill overtook her body. Was he a cheater, like Brad? Had he been two-timing her? But why was Tori saying she was here to see *both* the brothers?

Melissa resumed pacing. How could Sergei be seeing both she and Tori? He'd been spending a lot of time with Melissa. But they'd never talked about being exclusive. As a matter of fact, Melissa had assumed until their discussion yesterday that they were more "friends with benefits" and she'd told him so. If she was just that then he didn't owe allegiance to her.

Sergei had said he cared, that he wanted something more. Had she put too much emphasis on his words?

She needed to confront him and see what he had to say.

She went back to the front window again and peered out. The garage and driveway lights were bright, and revealed that Tori's car was still there. Melissa could hear its motor purring.

She stood there for a good five minutes. Finally as she watched, Sergei's truck pulled into the driveway, slowing as it passed Tori's car. A black truck followed Sergei's blue one. That was most likely Dennis'.

Sergei must have recognized Tori in her car, because he lowered his window and Tori must have done the same. The woman called out something to Sergei, something Melissa couldn't hear, and he answered, then passed her and continued down the driveway and parked out of Melissa's line of sight, followed by the other truck.

Melissa felt a strong impulse to leave the scene. She didn't want to witness an argument, or to see him with Tori. She was about to grab her coat when the voice inside her brain commanded *"wait a minute, girl."*

Why should she run out on Sergei and Tori? She had done nothing wrong. As a matter of fact, she should be demanding to know what was going on after the evening had been disrupted by this—this nutty female. She had thought after yesterday that she and Sergei had an—an understanding, at least.

She stepped away from the closet and waited in the living room. Looking out the window, she saw Sergei had exited from his truck, and Dennis was doing the same. They met Tori by her car as she slid out, and then the three turned toward the house.

Melissa plopped down on the sofa and waited.

They entered, and she heard Dennis say something to Sergei in Russian over Tori's head.

They all took off their coats, and Tori handed hers to

Sergei. He didn't hang it in the closet with his; but dropped it over a nearby chair.

As Melissa watched she didn't say a word. Sergei and Dennis both looked at her; they must have seen the annoyance and simmering anger on her face.

She expected Sergei to say something like "I can explain" but he didn't. He turned to Tori. "What are you doing here?"

She widened her eyes. "Didn't Dennis tell you I called him?"

Relief hit her so hard Melissa felt like an electrical shock had zapped her body.

What? Why did this whole scene matter to her? Wasn't Sergei just a lover to her, a booty-call? She had made it clear to him she wanted a no-strings-attached affair. She didn't want emotional involvement.

But she was--emotionally involved, that is!

She sat up straight as shock waves vibrated through her. Despite her original desires, despite all her wishes, she *did* care about Sergei. Like him, she had developed feelings. As the shock waves pummeled her, she stood. She felt her body begin to tremble.

Sergei sent her a beseeching glance. "Wait, Melissa. Give me a chance to clear this up."

She sat back down. And listened, observing carefully not simply the words, but their body language. Her thoughts continued to whirl. She cared about Sergei! Despite the barriers she'd put up, she had feelings. And right now she felt hurt.

"Didn't you tell your brother I called?" Tori was demanding, putting a hand on Dennis's arm. She looked up at him, then turned to look hopefully at Sergei.

Dennis' face reddened. "I—I meant to…"

Sergei turned towards Dennis. "She called you?" He sounded surprised.

Dennis at least looked embarrassed. "Yes. A few days ago. She wants a chance to talk to Mom. I always thought Tori was a talented artist—and so did Victor, by the way," he defended himself to Sergei. "I invited her here so we could put our heads together and see if Mom could help her. You know, Mom has become acquainted with a few gallery owners in the last couple of years."

Sergei nodded.

Had they forgotten that she was here? Melissa wondered.

"Isn't Hanukkah supposed to be the season of miracles?" Tori asked the guys, looking from one to the other. Her voice sounded imploring.

"Yeah…" Sergei sounded reluctant as he looked at her. "But I told you my mother has no influence."

"But she might," Dennis contradicted. "Let's see what Tori wants and get mom on the phone. This could be a break for her."

Melissa must have made an unconscious sound, or something, because the brothers turned to stare at her.

"You can, Dennis." Sergei said. "I want to talk to Melissa. Alone."

CHAPTER X

Sergei strode towards Melissa. Grabbing her hand, he asked her, "please come with me." As she hesitated, he repeated, "please," and gave a small tug.

She let him lead her wordlessly to his bedroom.

He'd tried to straighten it up. He'd made the queen-sized bed but he caught sight of his worn sneakers sticking out from underneath.

Now he ran his hand through his hair. "Sit down. Please."

She sat in a chair by a desk and he sat near her on the bed.

"Melissa—" he began, "I never expected to see Tori again. I guess you heard what Dennis said—that *he* invited her here."

"Yes, but—" she looked perturbed. "I could see—the way she looks at you—she still has feelings for you, Sergei."

He could see the doubt clouding her expressive face.

"I care nothing for her," he clipped out. "Can't you see, Melissa?"

He knew he had to convince her. She'd been betrayed and hurt in the past—he had to prove that he could be trusted. "Please believe me." He leaned over and pulled her onto his lap

She took a deep breath. "I—I realized when I was

sitting there—I care about you too, Sergei—a lot. Maybe—maybe love." She spoke hesitantly, breathlessly.

Happiness flashed through his entire body. He hugged her tightly. "Melissa!" Those were words he'd hoped to hear.

He kissed her, hard. "I love you," he repeated on a ragged breath.

"Oh, Sergei…" She threaded her fingers in his hair.

Their kiss flared to life and they slid together on the bed.

***

This wonderful guy loved her! And she was becoming more and more convinced she had those same feelings for him. Melisssa felt almost dazed by these revelations. They kissed each other intensely, and she was barely conscious of anything but the overwhelming realization of her own astounding feelings for this incredible, considerate and sexy man.

When he began to fondle her breast, she suddenly became self-conscious. "Sergei," she whispered, her hand unable to resist stroking his chest, "The—the others—they're in the living room—"

He groaned, then stood up and walked to the door. Locking it, he turned back to her, a grin on his face. He slid down beside her and took her into his arms. "Now, where were we…?"

"Right here," she replied firmly. "Just where we should be." She kissed him passionately to show him her awakening love.

Afterwards, they lay blissfully tangled together.

"Happy Hanukkah, Melissa," he whispered.

She wove her fingers with his. "Happy Hanukkah, Sergei." It sounded like a pledge.

EPILOGUE

Hanukkah, the following year

We're going to light the menorah, everyone! Gather around!" Melissa's sister Courtney called the group together.

They gathered inside Courtney and Ben's large living room.

Her sister held a box of matches. The shiny menorah stood in the middle of the table, with one candle and the shamash candle to light it for the first night of Hanukkah.

Melissa looked around. Her family—both of her sisters and their husbands, her parents, Ben's family, plus Sergei's—had come here to Courtney and Ben's huge house, to celebrate the holiday. She was so grateful to everyone there that they'd all managed to clear their busy schedules to be together for the first night of Hanukkah.

Sergei's arm tightened around her shoulders. She felt as if she was glowing like the candles, secure in his love. She joined in as the collective group chanted the traditional blessing and Courtney lit the shamash, then the first night's candle.

"I have a question," Sergei said loudly.

"Questions are part of the Passover seder," Melissa's

sister Sherry joked. "You got the wrong holiday!" But a wide smile lit her face.

Sergei removed his arm, and pivoted to stand before Melissa. He dropped to one knee.

Melissa stared at him. Suddenly her heart began to hammer and her pulse went haywire. *Was he about to--*

"Melissa, I love you," he started, his face earnest. "Totally. I want to spend my life with you." His words were solemn. Then he smiled. "Will you marry me?"

Tears sprang to her eyes. "Oh, Sergei!" She dropped down beside him on the floor and hugged him. "Yes!"

Everyone burst into applause. Added in were shouts of "Congratulations!" and "Mazel Tov!" Flashes shone as a dozen cameras snapped photos.

Melissa and Sergei hardly noticed. They were too busy kissing.

THE END

ABOUT THE AUTHOR

Roni Paitchel Denholtz has been writing and publishing for over 40 years. Her short stories, articles and poems have been published in national and regional magazines such as True Romance, Child Life, Modern Romance, For the Bride and Baby Talk. She is the author of nine children's books published by JANUARY PRODUCTIONS, an educational publisher. Her book "Jenny Gets Glasses" was named to the Favorites of First Graders list by the Reading is Fundamental group, which was spearheaded by the late Barbara Bush.

She has published 25 romance novels, beginning with "Lights of Love," published by Avalon Books. Her romance novels have been nominated, and won, many prestigious fiction awards, such as the NJ Golden Leaf award and the National Readers' Choice awards. She is especially known for the award-winning LIGHTNING STRIKES series, a paranormal series with characters who have ESP and other psychic abilities.

In her "everyday life" she was a special eduction teacher in Dover, NJ teaching reading and math to children with learning disabilities and other handicaps while earning her M. A. and writing on the side. She then became a realtor and wrote part time. She has also done volunteer work in PTA, Marching Band parents and

Robotics parents, plus she served on the board of her local animal shelter for 8 years, helping to save and rehome dogs, cats and even guinea pigs. She also taught "Writing for Fun and Profit" in her local adult school and many of her students have gone on to publish articles, poems and books.

Roni and her husband and their dog make their home in beautiful northwest New Jersey. Their daughter and son are grown and married, and she is now a proud grandmother.

You can find Roni often on Facebook, under Roni Denholtz, Author Roni Denholtz and The Lightning Strikes series. She is also on Instagram.

Please visit her webpage at www.ronidenholtz.com and sign up for her newsletter!

BOOKS BY RONI DENHOLTZ

The Lightning Strikes Series
Lightning Strikes
Lightning Strikes Again
Lightning Strikes Twice
Lightning Strikes the Billionaire
Lighting Strikes Anew

Historicals
Marquis in a Minute
One of These Nights
One of These Wylder Nights

"Sweet" Contemporaries
Lights of Love
Somebody to Love
Negotiating Love
Salsa with Me
A Taste of Romance
Setting the Stage for Love
Room for Love
Forecast for Love

Contemporary Romance
Borrowing the Bride

Contemporary Romance Novellas
Stuck in the Saddle with You
Those Canyon Nights
Return to Forever
Eight Nights to Win Her Heart
Enchanted Vermont Nights
Meet Me at the Inn
Eight Nights of Apricot Cookies
Chocolate Caramel Dreams
One Hot Hanukkah

www.ingramcontent.com/pod-product-compliance
Lightning Source LLC
Chambersburg PA
CBHW060504300726
48975CB00008B/2638